"Are You Trying To Impress Me?"

"Until this moment, I hadn't thought so," Evan responded.

"Well, you're succeeding," Anna told him in a mock whisper.

Laughing, he rose from his chair and held his hand out for her. "Dance with me?"

But their laughter stopped when he took her in his arms, when their bodies touched, when he led her in the timeless, graceful steps of the waltz.

Anna had loved him before tonight, had known it with a surety that shocked her defensive, shock-resistant heart. And she had wanted him before, had known it with a surety that went beyond any reason.

But after this exquisite, torturous closeness, she thought she would probably die if they didn't act on the desire thrumming through her body.

Dear Reader,

Readers ask me what *I* think Silhouette Desire is. To me, Desire love stories are sexy, sassy, emotional and dynamic books about the power of love.

I demand variety, and strive to bring you six unique stories each month. These stories might be quite different, but each promises a wonderful love story with a happy ending.

This month, there's something I know you've all been waiting for: the next installment in Joan Hohl's *Big, Bad Wolfe* series, July's *Man of the Month, Wolfe Watching*. Here, undercover cop Eric Wolfe falls hard for a woman who is under suspicion.... Look for more *Big, Bad Wolfe* stories later in 1994.

As for the rest of July, well, things just keep getting hotter, starting with *Nevada Drifter*, a steamy ranch story from Jackie Merritt. And if you like your Desire books fun and sparkling, don't miss Peggy Moreland's delightful *The Baby Doctor*.

As all you "L.A. Law" fans know, there's nothing like a good courtroom drama (I *love* them myself!), so don't miss Doreen Owens Malek's powerful, gripping love story *Above the Law*. Of course, if you'd rather read about single moms trying to get single guys to love them—*and* their kids—don't miss Leslie Davis Guccione's *Major Distractions*.

To complete July we've found a tender, emotional story from a wonderful writer, Modean Moon. The book is titled *The Giving*, and it's a bit different for Silhouette Desire, so please let me know what you think about this very special love story.

So there you have it: drama, romance, humor and suspense, all rolled into six books in one fabulous line—Silhouette Desire. Don't miss any of them.

All the best,

Lucia Macro
Senior Editor

Please address questions and book requests to:
Silhouette Reader Service
U.S.: 3010 Walden Ave., P.O. Box 1325, Buffalo, NY 14269
Canadian: P.O. Box 609, Fort Erie, Ont. L2A 5X3

MODEAN MOON
THE GIVING

SILHOUETTE *Desire*®
Published by Silhouette Books
America's Publisher of Contemporary Romance

SILHOUETTE BOOKS

ISBN 0-373-05868-3

THE GIVING

Copyright © 1994 by Modean Moon

This edition published by arrangement with Harlequin Enterprises B. V.

® and TM are trademarks of Harlequin Enterprises B. V., used under license. Trademarks indicated with ® are registered in the United States Patent and Trademark Office, the Canadian Trade Marks Office and in other countries.

Printed in U.S.A.

MODEAN MOON

once believed she could do anything she wanted. Now she realizes there is not enough time in one life to do everything. As a result, she says her writing is a means of exploring paths not taken. Currently she works as a land-title researcher, determining land or mineral ownership for clients. Modean lives in Oklahoma on a hill overlooking a small town. She shares a restored Victorian farmhouse with a six-pound dog, a twelve-pound cat and, reportedly, a resident ghost.

One

"**O**hmygod."

The single word was no more than a whisper, a mutter, a prayer, before the liquid from the straw struck Anna's throat, definitely the wrong way, and she had to focus all her attention on fighting a cough that threatened to turn into a really nasty attack.

Served her right, she thought when she had her breathing once again under control. Years before she had realized how futile it was for her to look at men, sexy or not, so she had stopped—except for that one disastrous time, which had only proved that she was an absolute idiot even to consider looking, hoping, dreaming.

So the fact that the sexiest man she had ever seen had just happened to walk into Anna's hospital room should have had no effect on her whatsoever—wouldn't have, she told herself, if she hadn't been affected more than she'd thought by her enforced inactivity. But he *had* walked into her room, with all the assurance of someone who owned not only the room, but the entire hospital. And she *was* affected by the lean dark looks of a complete stranger.

He spared a glance for her. She watched hazel eyes fringed with incredible lashes widen before he masked his surprise, or dismay, and turned impatiently toward the door.

His impatience wasn't for her, Anna realized, but for the tall, slender, dark-haired woman who followed him.

Anna let herself look at women, analytically, critically, and sometimes, when she was feeling especially vulnerable, enviously. This woman was beautiful; no one could deny that. But it was a brittle kind of beauty, the kind that was always carefully creamed and pampered and prepared for viewing. And it was a mature beauty. How much older was she than her companion? Ten years? More? Less? It was hard for Anna to judge.

The woman looked at Anna and then averted her gaze as she swept regally to the second bed. The man placed a beautifully crafted leather suitcase on the bed tray and reached for one of the curtains that separated the beds.

"Excuse me," he said, but Anna recognized it for the perfunctory statement it was and realized that he forgot her presence as soon as he closed the curtain surrounding the new arrival's bed.

Anna would have smiled, had she been able to. Here she was, wrapped up like the Invisible Man, and that was exactly how she was being treated—as though she were invisible. Well, that suited her just fine. It was, in a way, a kinder response than she was used to receiving from men. And it freed her to fantasize about the man on the other side of the curtain, and to eavesdrop blatantly on his conversation with her new roommate. Both actions were alien pastimes to her, but infinitely preferable to worrying about the outcome of her surgery, scheduled for the next morning.

Sexy, she thought. Yes, he was definitely that. She'd sculpt him in bronze, if she sculpted him, because that was the only medium that could capture the sleekly molded muscle and sinew she sensed beneath his well-tailored three-piece suit. She shook her head against the pillow. A three-piece suit. No one wore a three-piece suit in Van Buren, Arkansas, in August. Well—she amended her thought—almost no one. But she could forgive him that; he hadn't looked the least bit wilted.

Age was something she wasn't very good at guessing. If he was as old as the woman who accompanied him, he'd have some trace of gray in his hair, but he didn't. It was a thick, lustrous black, with a natural sheen to it that could never have come from a bottle. So. He was definitely younger. But how much? That, she supposed, depended on how old the woman was. There were lines of experience stamped on his face. They didn't detract from his good looks, but they were there just the same. Thirty-five, she decided. Thirty-five to Anna's twenty-eight. A little bit of an age difference, but not much. Yes. A nice age. Especially if she was just indulging in fantasy.

His height? A little over six feet, she estimated, although she knew she had to allow some margin for error because of her horizontal position. But she'd definitely be able to wear her highest heels with him and not have to worry about his ego.

And he didn't carry any extra weight. She had seen no sign of a beer drinker's belly or a pencil pusher's backside on his lean frame.

He was someone who was used to spending a lot of time outdoors, Anna decided, caught up in her unaccustomed musings. In spite of that pompously expensive dark suit. Because although his complexion was probably naturally dark, it was sun-deepened to a shade only a little lighter than the bronze image she could already see taking shape.

But he was taken, she reminded herself. Taken by an extremely beautiful woman.

As if that made any difference. Taken or not, he would never be attracted to her.

The game had palled for Anna, but just as she decided she no longer wanted to play, she realized she had no choice, at least as far as eavesdropping was concerned.

The noises from the other side of the room had been inconsequential—the snapping of luggage locks, the whisper of clothing, footsteps. Now Anna heard the bathroom door open and, through the opening in the curtain, saw the woman, a vision in a red satin robe, walk from the bathroom toward her bed. There was the click of a cigarette lighter, a long exhalation, then the aroma of tobacco. And, finally, voices. And no matter how Anna tried to shut them out, no matter how softly the other two spoke, the fact was that they stood only a few feet from her, separated from her by no more than a thin layer of fabric.

"Eileen." The man's voice was deep, well modulated, the voice of someone used to giving orders. "You still have time to change your mind."

"Why, darling boy..." The woman's laugh, and her voice, were as cultivated as her beauty. "Why on earth would I want to do a thing like that?"

"Because this isn't necessary."

"Necessary for whom?" Eileen asked, and all traces of laughter disappeared. "For you?"

Anna heard the rustle of satin and knew the woman had settled herself on the bed.

"No. You wouldn't understand would you, Evan? When you are my age, you still won't understand. But then, when you are my age, women will call you 'rugged-looking' and 'maturely handsome.' Do you know that men have thicker skins than women? Literally, as well as figuratively. It isn't fair, but men don't show age the way women do, and no one, *no one*, will ever say of you, 'Isn't it a shame the way his looks have gone to hell?' or 'He used to be a real beauty. Pity, isn't it?' So don't tell me what's necessary, Evan. Just help me get through this, and make my excuses until I'm fit to be seen in public again, and then we'll talk about what *you* want. We both know you're not here because of undying love, but for now, at least, I hold all the cards.''

"That's going to be a problem, isn't it, Eileen?'' the man asked, apparently deciding to ignore what had sounded to Anna like an attempt at a fatal barb. "Helping you get through this? I can't see you being satisfied with anything less than a private room, with anything less than a prestigious hospital facility, with anything less than *cordon bleu* food.''

"Yes,'' she interjected, "it is a problem. But William Hatfield is the best surgeon in this part of the country. If he chooses to operate in this backwater facility, then I have no choice but to endure it. And if I am to be completely healed in time for the holidays, I have no choice but to endure it now, whether there is a private room available or not.''

Anna heard no distinguishable reply from the man.

"And that frightful creature in the opposite bed is not going to bother me. Well,'' Eileen admitted wearily, "she will bother me—anyone bandaged that completely would naturally bother me—but she will not intrude on my privacy. I simply will not allow it.''

That creature in the opposite bed wouldn't dream of intruding on your privacy, Anna thought, turning her face to the pillow. *And you'd damn well better not intrude on mine.*

Frightful? Maybe she was, with her head wrapped up like a mummy. But *creature?*

That's what you get for eavesdropping, she told herself, but the thought brought her no comfort. And what had she learned in exchange for that painful impression? Names. Evan and Eileen. Two perfect names for two perfect people. Perfect, if all one measured perfection by was wealth and beauty. And that Eileen was not satisfied with her beauty. William Hatfield *was* the best surgeon in his field in this part of the country. Anna knew that, because Bill was her doctor, too. And his field was cosmetic and reconstructive surgery.

"Eileen, will you please lower your voice," Evan said softly. "That is a curtain, not a wall."

Any reply Eileen might have made was silenced by the entrance of Kate Dobbins. Anna recognized Kate's voice and straightened her head on the pillow. There wasn't any point in inviting a lecture from Kate, no matter how gently it was given, and if Kate thought Anna was skulking or depressed, there would be a lecture.

"Hello, Mrs. Claymore," Kate said pleasantly. "I'm Dr. Dobbins, your anesthesiologist."

Anna reached for the call panel and switched on the television. She'd learned her lesson when it came to eavesdropping. She ran through the channels until she found an old movie, then placed the pillow speaker next to her ear. But no matter how hard she concentrated on Gary Cooper's voice, she couldn't close out all the conversation from across the room.

Anna heard things that were a definite intrusion on Eileen Claymore's privacy. Like her age. Fifty-eight. In spite of knowing that it could be of absolutely no importance to her, Anna found herself again speculating on the relationship of the two persons across the room. Could she have misread that relationship? Then the significance of the numbers penetrated Anna's bemused consciousness. *Fifty-eight*, for God's sake, and the woman was dissatisfied with her appearance?

Still bemused, Anna remained an unintentional intruder. And the facts continued to roll through the fragile barrier of the curtain—that this was Eileen Claymore's third surgery...that the last one had been done ten years before...that Evan's last name was the same as Eileen's....

"So," Kate said, shuffling the papers in her hands, "I'll see you in the morning. You're scheduled for ten o'clock, right after Anna—Miss Harrison. Both of you are going to be feeling pretty rotten tomorrow afternoon, but in your case that will soon pass. Any questions?"

There were no questions, only a round of polite good-byes. Anna heard Kate pause beside her curtain. Then Kate stepped inside the enclosed area and walked to the side of Anna's bed. She was still in scrubs, and she wore a paper shower cap on her mop of dark curls and paper covers on her shoes.

"Hi, Anna. Any problems?"

"No," Anna said through her teeth. It wasn't impossible for her to speak, just difficult, but then, she and Kate had been through this before. "Who are you trying to impress with your costume?"

Kate laughed and reached for Anna's hand. "Good girl. I was afraid you might be hiding in here brooding. Are you ready for tomorrow?"

Anna squeezed Kate's hand.

"Fine," Kate said. "I know Dr. Hatfield has already talked with you. I know you know what to expect. You're scheduled for first thing in the morning, so I'm going to put you to sleep a little early tonight. Any objections?"

"No," Anna told her. "Now, if you want. I'm not looking forward to the wait."

"Then let me give you something to look forward to," Kate said gently. "If all goes as well as we expect, you'll soon be eating real food. Something solid. Like Jell-O."

Anna choked on a laugh, and Kate leaned close, conspiratorially. "Have you seen that gorgeous man on the other side of the curtain?" she whispered.

Anna glanced at her warily.

"Well, I'm going to leave the curtain open just a little when I go, so that you can look at him some more."

"Kate! No!"

Kate winked at her. "Kate, yes. There's nothing like a little healthy lust to take your mind off your problems." She straightened from the bed and grinned wickedly. "So, Miss Harrison," she said in a normal voice, "if you have no more questions, I'll see you in the morning."

True to her word, Kate opened the curtain at least another foot as she stepped from behind it. And she left it open. Anna couldn't see the opposite bed through the opening, but she could see the chair where Evan Claymore sat with his head thrown back and his tie loosened.

Healthy lust? Anna wasn't sure *healthy* was the right adjective. But lust? If that was what this tingling awareness of his masculinity was, if that was what caused the tightening in her stomach, the almost painful awareness of the starched sheet across her breasts, the sense of frustrated anticipation she felt when she looked at him, then lust certainly could take one's mind off one's problems. The only thing that spoiled it for her was the knowledge that at any moment he might turn his head and look at *her*.

Evan hated waiting, had hated it ever since he was a child and had no control over his own actions. Now, it seemed to him, he had been thrust back in time by a quirk of Eileen's perfectly arched eyebrow and the promise that—for a few weeks, at least—she needed him. That, and the fact that she held the fate of his family's trucking company in her perfectly manicured hand—held it like a carrot in front of him. *Be good, darling boy, and maybe Mommy will love you. Be good, darling boy, and maybe Mommy will let you have this toy you want so much.*

Evan twisted his neck, attempting to shake off the exhaustion caused by too little sleep, attempting to shake off the cynicism that had settled over him like a shroud the past few years.

He hated waiting. He went back to that thought. That was an acceptable complaint. But if he had to wait—and he did have to, he admitted—the unoccupied hospital room, with its two freshly made beds, was preferable to the enforced intimacy of the crowded waiting rooms near Surgery.

He glanced across the room. The other woman—Anna Harrison, Dr. Dobbins had called her—had already been taken to Surgery by the time he arrived that morning. And it was just as well. He hadn't thought it possible, but even medicated, Eileen had been even more demanding than the night before.

He glanced from one to the other of the two waiting beds, as if they could tell him why women subjected themselves to this sophisticated form of torture. Eileen's would be almost finished by now. Her doctor had assured them it would be an uneventful procedure—a little tuck here, a little lift there, a little abrasion to renew the complexion.

Evan shuddered. A knife was still a knife, no matter how lightly one spoke of how it cut. How could women like his mother and her heavily bandaged roommate have let their vanity get so out of control that they willingly submitted to "a little tuck, a little lift" instead of gracefully accepting the natural process of aging? No, he thought, remembering Eileen's words of the night before, he would probably never understand why, even if he was intimately familiar with the type of woman who did.

He heard the soft *whoosh* of the room's door opening and looked up to see the roommate being brought back into the room on a gurney. Efficiently the team lifted her onto the bed and settled patient, IV bottle and assorted paraphernalia in place.

After the rest of the team left the room, a nurse looked around the room and then at Evan. "Have you seen Lisa—Anna's sister?"

Evan shook his head.

"Damn! She promised me—" Apparently remembering her sleeping patient, the nurse stepped closer to Evan, lowering her voice. "Look, I can't stick around right now, and this place is a madhouse, so we can't really spare anyone else. It looks like you're going to be here anyway, so you're elected. Anna's going to be drifting in and out of lullaby land for a while, and she's going to be thirsty. No water, understand. But if she asks, there's crushed ice in that container. Give her a little—just a small amount. Put a part of a spoonful between her lips. And push the call button if you think she's in serious distress. Thanks. Bye."

Evan stared after the nurse's retreating back in dismay. Unless he was mistaken, he'd just been drafted as a baby-sitter for a complete stranger. And what in the hell did she mean by serious distress, anyway?

Stubbornly determined that he wouldn't be forced into nursemaiding a second woman through the aftereffects of elective surgery, Evan turned his back to her. He walked to the window and looked out at the gentle hills that marched upward from the wide valley of the Arkansas River to the Boston Mountains, in the heart of the Ozarks.

He didn't object to giving care to anyone. In fact, he recognized a deeply buried need in him to give care, to give love. But he hated like hell to have anything forced on him. And in spite of all he had tried to tell himself about Eileen finally needing him, he knew she didn't really need *him*, didn't want *him*—just someone to wait on her.

A low moan dragged Evan's attention back to the hospital room, prodding his conscience. He couldn't ignore the woman. Even when it was unnecessarily invited, pain was still pain. He wouldn't nursemaid her, but he could at least summon someone to help her.

Her eyes were open—open and watching him as he reached across her face for the call panel that had been fastened to her pillow. Her eyes were dark, sooty, fringed with heavy lashes, and slightly unfocused, but he saw no fear in them, only a mild questioning alarm at finding a stranger leaning over her. Most of all, he saw no imperious demand in them.

Evan stopped reaching for the call panel. "Are you thirsty?" he asked softly.

Her head was still swathed in bandages, but somehow they didn't seem as bulky as they had the day before. Her lips were visible—soft, full, a pale pink. He watched as the tip of her tongue eased out to moisten them—they parted, closed, then tilted slightly, as if in a smile.

"Yes . . . please."

Unexplainably touched by what was surely nothing more than a trick of the light, Evan picked up the container of ice.

"The nurse said no water," Evan told her as he dipped the spoon into the container.

"I know."

Gently he slipped a few slivers of ice from the spoon past her lips. She sighed and relaxed against the pillow, still watching him with those incredible eyes. *God,* he thought, *even her eyes are smiling.* A trick of the light, he surmised. A fluke.

Her lips moved again as she captured the ice more firmly. "Thank you," she said.

How had she done that? Evan wondered. She'd spoken, almost clearly, without any visible movement. "How did you do that?" he asked, surprising himself with his rudeness. But she didn't notice. Anna Harrison was once again asleep.

He'd watch her the next time, Evan decided, not realizing that he had gone from refusing to help this stranger to accepting that there would be a next time.

But there wasn't. As Evan waited for Anna to wake again, to see those incredible eyes, just to prove to himself he had been mistaken about seeing a smile in them, gentle or otherwise, a steady stream of hospital employees made their way into the room and to Anna's bedside. Nurses, aides, orderlies, clerical employees wearing hospital ID. There were so many that Evan lost count. When Anna was asleep, the current visitor would pat her hand, smooth her sheet or her pillow, linger a moment before leaving. When she was awake, the visitor would spoon ice chips past her lips, and always Anna would respond with either a pat of her hand, a smile, or a softly murmured thanks.

Incredible, Evan thought. Half the staff of the hospital must have been in this room. Why? What hold did this woman have over them? Whatever it was, no one seemed to object. Each person seemed to care genuinely for the now-sleeping woman.

He recognized Kate Dobbins, the anesthesiologist, when she entered the room and walked to Anna's bedside. After a few moments of standing silently by the bed, holding Anna's hand, Kate smoothed the already smooth sheet and walked toward Evan.

"Mrs. Claymore came through her surgery without any problem," she said, an unmistakable reserve in her voice that Evan hadn't heard the day before. "She is in the recovery room now, and should be brought back to the room in an hour or so. Dr. Hatfield had another surgery, but he will be up to talk to the both of you as soon as he's finished."

"Thank you. Dr. Dobbins?" he said when Kate turned to leave. "Who is Anna Harrison?"

Kate hesitated, cocking her head to one side and studying Evan silently. "The name doesn't mean anything to you?"

"No. Should it?"

Kate's lips thinned. She shook her head softly, almost sadly. "No. I suppose it wouldn't. She's a talented artist, Mr. Claymore. She supports herself by working as a potter—quite a good one—and she's established quite a reputation for her work. But those of us who know and love her realize that her lasting fame will come from her sculpture."

"There seem to be a lot of you."

"I beg your pardon?" Kate asked.

"Those who know and love her. Judging from the number of persons who have been in today to see her or do something for her."

"Yes." Kate glanced again at Anna. "Well, I must be going...."

"Why?" Evan asked. Almost without realizing he was speaking, he gave voice to his questions. "If she has talent, and friends, why does she find it necessary to... to go through *this?*"

Again Kate shook her head. "Where have you been for the last year, Mr. Claymore?"

Evan didn't understand the relevance of the question, but he saw no reason not to answer it. "Until two weeks ago, I was either in our Virginia office or in Europe, working on the negotiations for our international transport line."

"Rumor has it that you're trying to reacquire Riverland Trucking."

"Excuse me, Dr. Dobbins, but is there a connection between your question and mine?"

For the first time, Kate smiled. The smile was a rueful one. "I have to go now, Mr. Claymore. If you're going to be in town for the next few days, you might want to visit Anna's shop. It's on Main Street, in the restoration area, just west of Logtown Road."

The door opened, and two women wearing surgical scrubs entered the room. Although they walked to Anna's bedside, they looked toward Kate. "How's she doing?" one asked.

"Fine," Kate said, and hurried from the room, leaving Evan with still more unanswered questions.

The steady stream of well-wishers continued across the room, and eventually Eileen was brought back. She was still heavily sedated, drifting in and out of consciousness as Anna had been, bandaged as Anna was. But the similarities ended there, Evan thought, grateful that the private-duty nurse who had been engaged for Eileen would begin her duties in only an hour or so.

Because in Eileen's eyes he saw imperious demand. And in her voice he heard no trace of thanks. He'd pulled the curtain, isolating her bed, at her insistence. Now he wondered if he could just step beyond it, to the other side of the room, where maybe—just maybe—his ministrations would be appreciated.

Anna was dreaming. She knew it was a dream, although she didn't want to wake up. Idly she wondered why she was having this kind of reaction while coming back from the anesthesia, when she'd never had a similar one before. It didn't matter. She felt the smile that curved her lips and spread its gentle warmth through her entire body.

Evan Claymore was standing beside her bed, holding that ridiculous red ice bucket, spooning slivers of ice between her parched lips, asking if he could help her. A dream. And she knew she would wake from it with a vengeance. But not yet. Not just yet . . .

Two

Eileen was asleep. At last. Evan turned from the window and looked at his mother. In the day following her surgery, she had become more querulous, more petulant, more demanding. He found a smile for her private nurse, a grandmotherly-type who deserved better than the sharp side of Eileen's tongue.

"Why don't you take a few minutes, Mrs. Johnson? I'll be here if she needs anything."

"Thank you, Mr. Claymore. I believe I will go get a bite to eat."

He hadn't meant to stay the morning, only to visit a few minutes and make his escape. He had an appointment in Fort Smith in two hours, and—he glanced at his watch—forty-five minutes with the law firm that had represented his father's business interests for years. Evan might never know how Eileen had influenced his father to divide his shipping interests and leave the overland trucking line to her, but at

least she had agreed to sell it to him, and this time he was
going to act before she could change her mind again.

The woman across the room was quiet, wrapped up in the
solitude of her curtained cubicle. The stream of visitors had
stopped, but not before Evan noticed a strangely disturbing fact. While it seemed that nearly everyone connected
with the hospital had spent a few seconds at her bedside, he
had seen no one who wasn't connected with the hospital visit
her. No family. No close friends. No business associates.
Curious.

Without being truly aware of his actions, Evan found
himself outside his mother's curtained cubicle, his hand on
the partially opened curtain surrounding Anna Harrison's
bed. She had pulled the bed tray across her lap, and scattered a clutter of catalogues on the tray and over the bed,
but she lay back against the pillows.

Thinking she was asleep, Evan started to step back, but
then her eyes opened.

They do smile, he thought, caught up in the wonder of
that thought, and not questioning how someone so completely bandaged could be seen to smile. "May I come in?"
he asked.

She raised a hand to her mouth, seeming almost bemused, but when her fingers touched the bandages, she
jerked them away slightly.

"Yes," she said. "Of course, Mr. Claymore." Her voice
was soft, and a little husky, as though seldom used. "I . . . I
overheard your name. I'm sorry, but there isn't much privacy in one of these rooms."

Evan winced. He'd tried to impress that fact on Eileen,
but she had carried on for almost two days as if she were in
the private room she continued to demand. "I imagine
you've overheard a lot more than my name," he said,
thinking of his mother's rude comments. *Creature. Frightful.* "And for that, I'm sorry."

"Pain and fear affect people differently," Anna Harrison told him. "I'm sure that when your mother begins to feel better—"

Evan choked back a laugh. Eileen was only running true to character, but he didn't need to share that information with a stranger. "Thank you, Miss Harrison. You're more forgiving than I would be."

"Not really," she told him. "I'm . . . I've had a lot of experience with that kind of reaction. Some people can't help being . . . put off by . . . by a bizarre appearance."

So much pain. Evan heard it. He felt it. And then it was gone. Her eyes were smiling again. Her lips were smiling, too.

Inexplicably embarrassed by having witnessed her unguarded agony, Evan sought an excuse to leave. He noticed again the catalogs. "Am I interrupting you? If you're busy—"

"I should be," she said, gathering catalogs and stacking them neatly. "If I'm going to have a Christmas season at all, I need to start ordering stock. But I've discovered I'm really not up to it yet. I should have listened to Bill."

Bill? Who was Bill? One of the hospital staff? Or someone who felt comfortable enough to give this woman advice, but not comfortable enough to visit her? *None of your business, Claymore,* he told himself.

"Dr. Dobbins tells me that you're a potter," he said, "and that you have your own shop."

"Yes, well . . ." She shrugged. "Unfortunately, I don't have—and won't have—the inventory I need to carry me through the season. But I do have access to the work of some talented friends.

"And you, Mr. Claymore? I haven't seen you around town. Are you new to the area? Or just here for your mother's surgery?"

"Not exactly. I'm originally from Fort Smith, but I've been away for years."

"What brings you back?"

"Business," Evan said. "I'm . . ." Abruptly realizing he was about to blurt out all sorts of family secrets, Evan caught himself. Well, some of the secrets weren't exactly secret any longer. "I'm with World Parcel," he told her, editing the truth quite a bit. "I'm here to help with the negotiations to acquire Riverland Trucking."

"Oh." Once again Anna's hand went to her mouth. "Oh, my. How . . . how interesting."

Interesting? Hardly. He'd been up to his neck in balance sheets and regulations for the better part of the two weeks he'd been home, and the only thing *interesting* had been the knowledge he was at last rescuing the company that had been his family's first venture from the mismanagement that had almost destroyed it.

One other thing was proving to be interesting, too—this stranger with the smiling eyes.

"Evan!" The demand came clearly through two sets of curtains.

"Sorry," he said, feeling as rueful as the smile he gave the bandaged woman. "Maybe . . . maybe we can visit again?"

"Evan, are you over there with that . . . that person?"

Damn Eileen. "I'm sorry," he whispered.

Anna Harrison shook her head. "Don't be," she told him, in a soft voice meant to carry no farther than his ears. "*You* did nothing to be sorry for."

Anna sank back against the pillows. *Oh, dear.* What she had just learned about Evan Claymore was just as stunning as the fact that he had willingly sought out her company. Riverland Trucking. Could he know? Surely not. Surely not even the rich and beautiful could be that devious. Bill. She had to talk to Bill.

Evan left the dark-oak-and-ancient-leather-furnished offices of the Fairmont law firm in a cold rage. He'd hidden the extent of that rage from Tom Fairmont, but had been

unable to mask completely the fury that gripped him. No
wonder Eileen wanted to sell now. And no wonder Kate
Dobbins had looked at him so strangely when he asked her
about Anna Harrison.

And Anna? *How interesting,* she'd said when she learned
who he was. Damn straight, it was interesting. Captivating,
compelling, intriguing.

Holy hell! Hadn't Eileen known he'd have to learn about
this? And had she truly not known who occupied the bed
across the room from her?

Evan took the Midland Avenue Bridge across the Arkansas River from Fort Smith to Van Buren and found the
turnoff to Main Street. Kate Dobbins had suggested he visit
Anna Harrison's shop on Main Street. Now he also understood that suggestion.

He parked at the top of the street, near the converted
railroad station, and walked down the hill through what
appeared to be a turn-of-the-century village. Restoration
work had started years before, and a Hollywood crew film-
ing a Civil War saga had completed at least the exterior
renovations, even installing modern streetlights that looked
like old-fashioned gas lamps.

Evan saw the board fence blocking the unsightly burned-
out ruins of one building first. Then he noticed the still-
boarded windows of the shop next door. The shop on Main
Street. Just west of Logtown Road.

Logtown Road, a state highway, stretched steeply to the
north from the downtown area. Trucks had long been pro-
hibited on the length of road leading into downtown Van
Buren, because of the sharp grade and the congestion in the
area.

According to Tom Fairmont, Anna Harrison had loaded
her van at the back of her shop, which was below her apartment, and then, apparently having forgotten something,
pulled into the loading zone in front of the shop. The driver
of the Riverland truck, disregarding the ban on using Log-

town Road, had lost his brakes on the hill and lost control of the truck at the Main Street intersection. The truck had struck Anna Harrison's van, knocking her through the window of her shop. The van had then come crashing into the building next door and burst into flames.

Evan reached out for the support of a streetlamp. It was as if he could hear the squeal of brakes, the screams, the crash of metal on metal, smell the fire. God! What terror she must have felt as she was hurled through space by the runaway truck.

And he had looked down on her because he thought she was giving in to vanity.

The words *reconstructive surgery* had taken on new meaning as Evan listened to Tom Fairmont describing the extent of Anna Harrison's injuries. Well, Evan had a few more injuries to add to that list—specifically the indignities to which she had been subjected because of Eileen's selfishness and lack of consideration.

He walked across the street to the shop entrance and found it locked, a small Closed sign taped to the plywood of the front door.

A woman setting out dried-flower arrangements in front of the shop on the other side of the street smiled at him.

"This is Anna Harrison's place, isn't it?" Evan asked, although the heaviness he felt crowding his chest needed no further confirmation.

The woman smiled. "Ah, yes. You're familiar with Anna's work?"

"Only by reputation."

"She'll be glad to hear that. Her sister's keeping the shop open for her—well, at least part of the time. Lisa's been spending a lot of time at the hospital the last few days. But she should be back soon, if you'd like to come back in, oh, an hour or so."

Lisa. The sister the nurse had asked about. The sister he hadn't seen at all. He wondered briefly where the sister was really spending her time, and then decided it didn't matter. He and Anna Harrison apparently had more in common than a mutual interest in a truck; they both had family that didn't bear too close scrutiny.

Evan shook himself away from the unpleasant thoughts of family, and the images of the wreck his active imagination had conjured up, and turned back to his car. A private room was definitely in order, he decided. And he would move heaven and hell to make sure one was made available. Not for Eileen—although he pitied anyone unfortunate enough to be assigned to share the room with her—but for Anna. Privacy was the least of the things his family owed her.

Anna was amazed at how fast everything happened. Bill had come to see her—as a friend, not a surgeon—and Eileen Claymore had assumed that William Hatfield was more interested in visiting *her*. She had summoned him to her bedside and then proceeded to complain loudly and bitterly about the constant interruptions of her rest caused by Anna's visitors and especially by Anna's "dreadful" appearance.

"This is a hospital," Bill had told her.

"I'm aware of that," Eileen had said. "And I believe I should be allowed to recuperate without being subjected to the trauma of having to look at that woman."

Anna had never seen Bill Hatfield so angry. She was quite sure that Eileen had not seen the expression on his face when he left the room, but Anna had. Within ten minutes, a pair of orderlies had come for Eileen Claymore and moved her to another room. Only after she was gone had Bill returned to visit Anna.

"I'm sorry about that," he told her.

Anna managed a soft chuckle. "People have been saying that to me a lot today," she told him.

"Oh? Who else?"

"Evan Claymore."

Bill took her hand in his. "You know who they are, don't you?"

"I do now," Anna said.

"I'm sorry. I had no idea she had been put in here with you until after surgery yesterday. She was on the waiting list for a private room. I'd hoped one would come up without my having to pull rank."

Anna heard the door open and looked up. Evan stood just inside the room, looking at his mother's empty bed, at Bill, who still clasped her hand consolingly, and finally at her. *He knows.* She closed her eyes against the recognition, and against the flicker of guilt she saw in his eyes. He hadn't known earlier—he had truly just been kind. She wished he didn't know now. But then, if wishes were wings she thought, remembering all the other platitudes she had learned as a child, there wouldn't be anything for him to know.

"My mother?" Evan asked, and Anna saw that Bill Hatfield wasn't the only one holding back anger.

"A private room became available," Bill told him.

Evan sighed and nodded. "May I speak with you, Dr. Hatfield?"

Anna squeezed Bill's hand. It was a silent signal to him to tend to Evan's questions. He smiled at her. "Grace has one more at home with the chicken pox, but as soon as Jason is noncontagious she'll be in to see you."

She nodded, but she couldn't look away from Evan's face, or rather from his eyes. *You were kind to me,* she wanted to say to him, tried to communicate to him without words. *And I'll always treasure that kindness. But I understand why it can't continue. I understand that under normal circumstances it would never have happened.*

Evan had wanted to talk to Bill Hatfield, but now he didn't know what to say. He paced the end of the hallway, trying to understand what he had seen in Anna's eyes in those few moments in her room, trying to sort through the feelings running rampant through him. He wasn't an emotional man—emotions had been burned out of him years ago—but something highly emotional had gripped him and refused to let him go. He couldn't even blame it on lust, since he had no idea how the woman behind those bandages looked. *Broken—that was how she looked.*

Evan stopped his pacing and sank onto one of the chairs placed in a comfortable grouping at the end of the hall. Bill Hatfield eased away from his studied slouch at the window and sat in the adjacent chair.

"I take it you just learned about Anna."

"Yes," Evan said. "How on earth did the two of them get put in a room together?"

"I don't know. I am certain it wasn't malicious."

"She shouldn't have been subjected to that."

"Mr. Claymore, your mother is a very resilient woman. I assure you—"

"Eileen? You think I'm concerned about Eileen?"

"Well, yes." Evan saw a reluctant grin cross Bill Hatfield's face before the doctor continued. "How did you find out?"

"That really isn't important," Evan said. "What is important is why I didn't find out sooner. I'm buying Eileen's interest in Riverland Trucking."

William Hatfield nodded. "I'd heard the rumor."

"Apparently everyone's heard the rumor. I'll be assuming all the company's liabilities."

Hatfield nodded.

"My attorney would probably advise me to keep my mouth shut at this point, but after what I learned today, I consider my obligation to Miss Harrison to be among those liabilities."

Again Hatfield nodded.

"I imagine her medical bills have been staggering."

"I think you'd better get to the point, Mr. Claymore."

Unable to sit still any longer, Evan sprang to his feet and began pacing. "Take it easy, Hatfield. What I'm trying to say is, you seem to be her friend, as well as her doctor. If there's anything she needs, I want you to let me know. There will be no skimping on our responsibility to Anna Harrison."

The next afternoon, Anna once again settled herself in with her wholesale catalogues. No one else had been assigned to the other bed in the room, so both sets of curtains were open and she was able to look out the windows at the wooded hillside. She had to get her Christmas stock ordered soon, but first she had to get some sort of inventory from Lisa.

Anna wondered where to draw the line between making allowances for Lisa's inability to cope with Anna's problems and throwing a good old-fashioned pity party for having no one close to her who *was* able to cope. For having no one close to her, period.

She couldn't cry. Not without getting into big trouble with Bill Hatfield and Kate Dobbins, not without getting into big trouble with herself, because Anna suspected that if she ever let down her guard enough to cry she wouldn't be able to stop.

Perverse creature that she was, she was even missing Eileen Claymore's presence in the bed across the room. *No, Anna,* she told herself, be honest. The person you miss is *Evan* Claymore.

And you can miss him until the world looks level, for all the good it will do you.

She pulled the catalogues to her chest and hugged them, realizing how long it had been since anyone had hugged her. Oh, there were pats and touches from her friends at the hospital, necessary, welcome, but right at this moment so insufficient.

A pity party, she thought. No. Not yet.

Sighing, she put the catalogues on the bed tray.

"That sounded serious."

She looked up. Her eyes widened, and she couldn't stop the silly smile she felt spreading through her. "Mr. Claymore."

"Evan," he told her, walking fully into the room. "May I come in?"

"Are you sure it's wise?"

He shook his head, and she saw the strangest expression in his eyes—a questioning, an acceptance, a disbelief. "No. I'm not sure at all."

Anna Harrison played cutthroat gin, cutthroat old maid, cutthroat any card game Evan suggested. And she laughed. Maybe it was her laughter that kept him coming back, afternoon after afternoon. Maybe it was the smile that lit her wonderful eyes. Maybe it was the ease with which she accepted his presence but never demanded it.

Come to think of it, Evan realized late that week, she never demanded anything. And maybe she ought to. He still hadn't seen Anna's sister, and Anna blocked any attempt at conversation in that area. And Anna still hadn't completed the catalogue orders; they sat in a neat stack on the table beside her bed.

"Gin," Anna said, laying down her cards.

"Again?" Evan chuckled and laid down his handful of cards. "You're going to have to count them this time."

"Okay." She picked up the cards and began counting them off. "Two hundred, three hundred, five hundred, a thousand."

"Hey..." he said, laughing. "Okay. Okay, I'll count my own cards. I didn't know you'd cheat me."

"Me?" Anna asked, laughing softly. "Never."

"No." Evan felt his laughter die. "I don't think you would, Anna." And he didn't. Anna Harrison was the most intrinsically honest person he had ever met, and the fact that such honesty was found in a woman compounded his surprise—his wonder—at having met her. "I think you must be the most beautiful person I have ever known."

Anna's hand flew to her bandaged face, and Evan saw her glorious eyes mist over.

He hadn't meant to hurt her, but somehow he had. Evan reached out and traced his fingers over her bandages. "These don't matter, Anna. I know you've been injured. I'm sorry for your pain. I'm sorry for the months that have been torn from your life. But Bill Hatfield is going to put you back together as good as new. You have to believe that."

Anna shook her head, but caught his hand to her face with her strong, long-fingered, graceful hand. He saw the tears glistening on her lashes, and something within him echoed the pain he felt in the tremor in her hand. "Anna...."

She shook her head again. "No. No, it's time for me to remember how to be honest. I've enjoyed your company so much, Evan—"

"That's a relief. I thought you were going to tell me something really bad."

"Please." She caught her lower lip between even white teeth, worrying it for a moment, before moving Evan's hand from her face.

"As good as new isn't very good," she told him. She opened the lid on the tray and took out a wallet, opening it. "Bill had a problem trying to rebuild my face," she said, "because I only have one picture of myself, and I only have that because it's required by law. He had to go by memory, and by imagination. I think you ought to see this before you spend much more time with me, Evan. I don't think I can hide behind these bandages any longer. It isn't fair to you. It isn't . . . it isn't fair to me."

She handed him her driver's license, with its small color photograph. The picture showed Anna with long, waving, tawny hair, clear, glorious dark eyes, fantastic bone structure, and—Evan closed his eyes as every one of Eileen's thoughtless cruelties returned to haunt him—covering the left side of her face, an enormous discolored birthmark.

"I'll take that back now."

Evan wanted to tell her that the birthmark didn't matter, but that would have been the worst kind of lie. It mattered; it had always mattered to her. He saw that in the defensive posture she had assumed, the shadows that clouded her eyes, the tremor in her voice that she tried and failed to hide. What made the birthmark even more obscene was the obvious beauty it covered.

Unbelievable, he thought as he handed her the driver's license, but being run over by a truck had been only another indignity in a long line of indignities. And there had been many—Evan knew that with certainty. And he now knew what had caused the pain he had sensed in her the day after her surgery.

He wanted to say something to comfort her, but he had no words sufficient for the grief her life must have contained. He wanted to hold her, but he knew that he, of all people, had no right to do so. He wanted to do *something,* but there was nothing he could do.

He picked up the stack of playing cards and counted out her points. "Ten, twenty, seventy . . ."

"Evan—"

"Okay. Ten, twenty, one hundred."

"Evan."

He dropped the cards and looked at her, swallowing his anger at the injustice life had dealt her. "You're still the most beautiful person I know, Anna. What else do you want me to say? That it's all right? It isn't. It's a travesty. It's a desecration. You should never have been forced to suffer as I know you must have. If I could do anything, *anything—*"

Anna caught his hand in hers, stilling his words, stilling him. "You have, Evan," she said softly, and he watched as the shadows fled from her lovely eyes, chased away by that impossible smile. "You have."

Three

Almost a week passed before Evan realized there *was* something he could do for Anna.

Briefly he wondered if he should talk to Tom Fairmont first, but he knew what the attorney would say: *Don't admit any more liability than you absolutely have to.* Well, Riverland *was* liable. A Riverland truck had torn apart Anna Harrison's life. The Claymore family *was* Riverland Trucking—had been for over a century and a half, since before the railroad came to this territory and freight was shipped either by riverboats or overland in heavy wagons, since an ambitious, slightly shady character by the name of Jed Claymore decided he could manage both methods of freighting more efficiently, and more lucratively, than anyone else.

Rumor and family gossip had Great-great-grandpa Jed using less than legal means to deal with his competition. Evan was quite sure Jed would not have been stopped in

anything he wanted to do by attorneys or questions of liability. And neither would Evan.

Another day passed before he was able to talk to Bill
Hatfield. Evan waited for him outside Surgery, walked with
him to the doctors' lounge and sat across from him while he
sipped at a cup of thick black coffee with enough sugar in
it to revitalize the dead.

"Didn't you take any nutrition classes in medical
school?" Evan asked wryly.

Hatfield gave him a weak smile, clasped the cup in both
hands and took another sip. "I've been in surgery for six
hours, I have an office full of patients to see, and I have a
cut-and-paste scheduled for two this afternoon. I don't have
time for nutrition."

Evan chuckled. "Do you have a few minutes to talk about
Anna Harrison?"

Hatfield sat a little straighter in his chair and peered over
the rim of the cup. "That depends on whether you want me
to talk as Anna's friend or as her doctor."

"Fair enough," Evan told him. "I'll talk to you as her
doctor. You decide how to answer. She showed me her
driver's license."

Hatfield plopped his cup on the table. "Why?"

"She seemed to think it would make some difference to
me."

"And did it?"

Evan felt the denial instantly, but almost as quickly came
a flash of unwelcome insight into himself. "I don't know,"
he said. "I've never seen her without her bandages. There's
an anonymity in that mask—maybe *mystique* is a better
word—that gave me the freedom to get to know Anna
without concern for how she looked."

"And now that you do know?"

"But I don't," Evan said. "I can't reconcile the woman I
know with that . . . that . . ."

"Monster?" Hatfield asked cautiously.

"No! My God, no! Never that! How could you even suggest such a thing?"

Hatfield shook his head. "What do you want from me, Mr. Claymore?"

"You're a cosmetic surgeon. You work daily making vain women more beautiful, repairing ravaged features. You put Anna's bones and skin back together. I want you to get rid of that—"

"Obscenity?"

"Yes. That's exactly what it is."

"Let me get this straight. You want me to put Anna back on the operating table, subject her to still more surgery, wave my magic scalpel and *fix* her? Why?"

That's a good question, Claymore, Evan thought. *Why indeed?*

"Dr. Hatfield, I'm not knowledgeable about reconstructive surgery. I will admit there was a time when I thought it was a frivolous field of medicine, but not anymore. I don't mean to belittle what you do, I just don't know the language to talk with you about it. Can anything be done to Anna's face to get rid of that birthmark?"

"Why?"

"Why? You're supposed to be her friend, man. You have to ask me why?"

"That's right. I have to ask you why. So Anna will look like someone you're not ashamed to be seen with?"

That wasn't the reason, was it? Once again Evan didn't truly like what he was seeing of himself. Maybe that was a small part of what had motivated him, but if so, it was such a small part that he hadn't been aware of it until Hatfield raised the question.

"Why?" Evan said softly. "Because Anna is a beautiful woman, inside, where it counts, and deserves to have the world know just how beautiful she is. Because I'm indirectly responsible for almost killing her, for ripping months out of her life while she recovers, for probably ruining her business. Putting her back where she was before this happened is not enough—not for her, and not for me. So, is there anything that can be done?"

Bill Hatfield remained silent for a few seconds, studying Evan, giving Evan enough time to realize that he had stated only a portion of his reasons, but not enough to realize what the whole of them was.

"Until recently," Hatfield said finally, "there was no effective treatment for that type of birthmark. Now, with the advent of laser surgery, there is."

"Are you familiar with the technique?" Evan asked.

"Yes."

"Does this hospital have the equipment you need?"

"Of course."

"Then do it."

"And tell Anna what?" Hatfield asked. "That you threw a little charity her way? Her pride wouldn't let her accept. Her pride wouldn't let her take the loan I offered her when the technique became available."

"Then don't tell her anything until it's over, and then, if you have to, tell her it was necessary if you were going to put her back in one piece. Surely you can come up with something, Hatfield."

For the first time that day, Bill Hatfield grinned. "I think I like you, Claymore. That's exactly what I did come up with, several surgeries back."

"You've done it already?"

"Of course I have. My wife and I love Anna Harrison like a sister. I wasn't about to get her in surgery and not take care of her. I donated my skill—neither you nor your insurance carrier will see a bill for that—but I might have to justify the charges for the equipment."

"Not to me."

"And not to Anna," Hatfield insisted. "She is never to know that it wasn't absolutely necessary."

He'd done it. Bill Hatfield had already done it. Anna wouldn't need more surgery. She'd never again have to flinch when someone looked at her picture. "She won't learn it from me," Evan promised.

"And she's not to know that I've removed the birthmark until her bandages come off. I don't want her worrying about the outcome—she doesn't need any more stress than she's already got."

"The business?" Evan asked. "The sister?"

Bill Hatfield grimaced. "Both of those are out of my control. Anna swears everything is all right. I only hope it is. In the meantime, promise you won't say anything to her."

Evan smiled as he extended his hand across the table. "I promise."

Anna stood at the window of her room, silent now, not truly aware of the passage of time. She had watched the hillside gradually darken, watched as scattered lights twinkled on against the encroaching darkness. Now lights from the hallway behind her intruded on her solitude. Trapped in the momentary mirror of her window, they threw images of the hospital at her, showing in slightly blurred clarity the activities in the hallway, while her image remained only a silhouette—a dark and lonely silhouette.

Visiting hours were almost over. She heard goodbyes from the hallway, muted promises to return, soft statements of love, of affection, of caring.

She lifted her hand to her cheek, touching the still tender skin, knowing it was still slightly reddened, as Bill had told her it would be for some time.

She was glad she couldn't see her reflection. If she couldn't see, perhaps she wouldn't have to face the changes this day had brought to her life.

She heard gentle laughter from somewhere down the hall and closed her eyes against a brief, bright burst of pain. Not everyone was alone.

She shook her head, denying the pain, denying her loneliness. She ran long fingers through her hair. It was soft, freshly shampooed, as well styled as she could manage until a trip to a stylist.

She wasn't alone. Not really, she insisted. She understood why Kate wasn't there; she was speaking at a medical conference in Houston. And Grace Hatfield still had a houseful of sick children. But Lisa? And Evan?

But she had no ties to Evan Claymore, no right to expect him to be with her tonight, to share with her this time of awesome contemplation about what would become of her life now.

She realized her hand had once again crept to her new cheek. She left it there, accustoming her fingers to the sensation of soft, unmarred skin.

Evan was a friend, nothing more. The hours they had spent together would always be precious to her, but they meant nothing. Nothing.

In all fairness to him, he *had* asked to be with her this afternoon when the bandages came off. She had made light of the event, rejected his offer. Vanity. She had wanted to postpone the time when he saw her as she really was. Now she wanted him to see her—wanted to see how he reacted to the newness of her face.

Fool, she thought as she leaned her head against the window glass. Fool. Fool. Fool.

"May I come in?"

He, too, was silhouetted against the lights of the hallway. But Evan's voice, the shape of him, the way he stood, were indelibly imprinted on Anna's memory. She turned slowly, not fully facing him, but looking toward the door.

"I'm sorry it's so late. I meant to be here earlier, but I got caught in an interminable meeting." He stepped inside the room, then hesitated. "Are you all right?"

"Yes." Anna spoke softly. "Yes, of course. I didn't expect you."

"I wouldn't have stayed away today, Anna. Surely you knew that."

And suddenly, for Anna, the night wasn't quite so dark.

Evan hesitated in the doorway, held silent by Anna's silence. She stood by the window, dressed in the same long, tailored dark blue robe he had seen draped across the foot of her bed countless times without recognizing the simple elegance of the fabric, without realizing the simple elegance of the woman who now wore it.

He'd known she was tall, known she was slender, known she hid her inherent fragility behind a facade of strength. He'd known all these things, but never before had that knowledge hit him with the force with which it now did as he watched her—hidden in shadows, outlined against the dark, defying the night.

She lifted her head, still not facing him, and drew a deep, sustaining breath.

"Yes. Yes, of course I knew that."

Slowly she turned toward him, her hand lifted, her chin jutting with a belligerence spoiled only by a slight tremor. The hallway lights revealed her eyes first, hesitant, questioning, and then the rest of her face.

Evan's breath caught in his chest. He'd suspected she would be beautiful, but the small, poorly focused photograph he'd seen had done nothing to prepare him for the vision she truly was. He'd seen her large dark brown eyes, with their long, sooty lashes, before. Her mouth, too—beautifully sculptured, smiling even in repose—he'd seen often. But the fine, delicate bones, the slim, aristocratic nose, the graceful lines of her throat beneath that obstinate chin, were all new to Evan, no longer hidden by a mask of bandages or a disguise of disfigured skin.

Without being aware of having moved, Evan found himself across the room, facing Anna. He lifted his hands to her face, catching his fingers in her short, spiky hair before moving them gently over her cheeks—both soft, both un-marred.

"My God," he whispered unsteadily. "I had no idea. Now even a blind man can see how beautiful you are, Anna Harrison."

"Do you think so, Evan?" she asked softly. "Do you really think so?"

Evan knew that nothing so simple as vanity prompted her question. He heard years of pain and rejection in her voice, and saw it in her eyes as they searched his. Then she was silent, waiting for his answer. And the silence screamed with all the tears she had never shed, all the words she had never spoken.

"How do I answer you?" he asked, uncertainly. "Since the first day, I've thought you were beautiful—inside, where it really matters. Now..." He shook his head. The mood had become much too heavy, much too intimate. "This face will only let the world in on the secret your friends have known for years."

He felt her tremble beneath his touch, saw the glimmer of hard-fought tears on her lashes. Hesitation, doubt and the memory of untold rejections still darkened her expressive eyes, but now those had been joined by something as necessary and as fleeting as hope, and Evan felt as though he had been given a glimpse of her soul.

"Oh, Anna, Anna..." he said, shared pain at the countless indignities she had suffered thickening his voice. He dropped his hands to her slender shoulders and felt the quiver that ran through her.

He shouldn't do this, he thought, shouldn't take the liberty of touching her, holding her. But if he didn't, who would? Where was the sister? Where were the friends? How long had it been since anyone—anyone at all—had held Anna Harrison, had given her the comfort of another person's touch?

As long as it had been for him.

Where the devil had that thought come from? Evan pushed it aside, along with unwelcome memories of meaningless touches, words, relationships. Tonight was for Anna.

Whispering her name, he gathered her to him. He felt her small start of surprise, of instinctive withdrawal, before she caught back a sob and surrendered against him.

She cried, quietly, furtively, at first, her face turned away from him but caught in the reflection in the glass as her tears streamed from her eyes.

How long, Anna? he thought. *How long since you've cried? How long since you've let anyone share your pain?* But he didn't say it, only whispered her name softly, repeatedly, as he stroked her back, her shoulders, the back of her head, until he felt the first sob break from her, and the next, and then he held her tighter, knowing she needed this—knowing that somehow he needed it, too.

Anna didn't know how long she cried. At first she tried not to, feeling a deep wave of embarrassment sweep over her for her weakness, for showing her vulnerability, for needs she doubted would ever—*could* ever—be met. Then the comfort enveloped her, the warmth of another person holding her close, lending her strength while she was weak, protecting her while she had no defenses with which to protect herself—giving her the illusion that he cared for her.

And then the embarrassment returned, slipped through her defenses, fortified them, and gradually, insistently, stiffened her body, silenced her sobs, stemmed the flow of her tears.

Anna drew a long, not-quite-steady breath and pulled away from Evan. And—almost reluctantly, it seemed to Anna in her emotionally fragile condition—he let her go.

"I'm sorry," she said quietly.

"Why?"

Why? Because she had indulged in what she'd always thought a luxury but was really as vital as breathing? Because she had allowed herself to accept care and comfort from another person? Because someone had been willing to give her that care and comfort?

She felt an impossible smile beginning, and an equally impossible lightness spreading through her.

"You're right," she said. "I'm not sorry. Thank you."

She felt his knuckle under her chin, lifting her face, felt the gentle touch of his fingers as he once again traced her cheeks, saw the steady concern in his eyes as he looked at her. He wasn't surprised. She hadn't known about the corrective surgery, but somehow Evan had. For a moment, all her defenses swarmed into action, prodded by an unreasonable guilt. She gave them a quick kick, sending them on their way. She had no reason to feel guilty.

"Bill said it was necessary," she told Evan, knowing he knew what *it* had to be.

Evan only smiled. "I'm glad. Does this mean you'll be going home soon?"

Home. Home to the welcoming nest she had made for herself over her shop. Except for brief visits, it had been months since she'd been there. Home to her shop, and her clay, and her wheel. Home to all the things that had given her life meaning.

"I think so," she said. "I still need a couple more releases, and I have to work out a home program with my physical therapist, but I should be going home within the week."

"In that case, Anna Harrison," Evan said solemnly, "I insist you let me be there for this milestone. I want to be the one to take you out of here."

Why? Why had she let herself succumb to weakness as she had? She never had before, and Anna promised herself she never would again. As for his taking her home, chances were something would come up to change his plans. After all, Evan was a friend—nothing more—and she knew from long experience that this was a truth she couldn't afford to forget.

* * *

Why had he opened his mouth and made himself vulnerable to such a potentially embarrassing situation? Evan had no business taking Anna home. He had no business seeing her outside the hospital. What he needed to do was distance himself from her so that when she sued Riverland Trucking, as he suspected she had every right to do, he wouldn't compromise either side by being caught in the middle, so that when she delivered the fatal blow to the already faltering company that had been Great-great-grandpa Jed's dream he wouldn't, no matter how wrongly, feel that she had betrayed him.

Two days later, on a bright, already sweltering late-August morning, Evan picked Anna up at the hospital and drove her, one small suitcase, two exotic-looking houseplants and a surprising bouquet of balloons to her home and shop on Main Street, just west of Logtown Road.

Anna sat quietly in the car after Evan pulled into the loading zone in front of her shop. Plywood in hasty but now well-aged patches greeted her, instead of the pleasant and tasteful window arrangements she had taken such pride in. The place looked abandoned. A few weeds, now dead and crumbling, had grown in cracked concrete near the door.

The scene was the same as it had been the last time she saw it, on a brief trip home from the rehab hospital, only shabbier.

The gaily decorated balloons from Kate Dobbins suddenly mocked her. Some homecoming. She gave herself a mental shake. She was home, and if that wasn't miracle enough, she was better than before. As for this old building, well, she had done wonders with it before, and she could again.

"Is something wrong?"

Anna thought of any number of ways she could answer Evan's question, but she heard the concern underlying his words, and she knew there was only one way to answer that. She turned to him, smiling, and saw a tentative answering smile in his eyes. "No," she said. "Nothing that can't be fixed, anyway. Well, yes," she admitted, grinning wryly, "I don't have my key to that new lock yet. Would you mind driving around to the back?"

Inside the shop, a heavy layer of dust covered the shelves in her storerooms, and empty cardboard boxes spewed forth shredded paper as though they had been prowled through by someone looking for the stock they no longer contained.

Anna looked around in dismay at her once orderly and well-stocked storeroom, but said nothing. She silently repeated the mantra she had adopted outside the building: "I've done wonders here before, I can do so again."

The next room contained her kilns, wheels and boxes of clay. The equipment was covered with the same heavy layer of dust, but needed only cleaning. And if no one had disturbed the clay since she put it away, it would be salvageable.

The next room was the smallest of the three main rooms on the ground floor. The plywood covering the doors and windows darkened the room, but tall, narrow windows fronting the second floor, as well as a pair of rooftop skylights, admitted light that filtered down through hazy, heat scented dust. The ceiling and the second-story floor had been skillfully removed in this area, opening it into a gracious and tasteful showroom. A beautiful old walnut staircase led up to a balcony that surrounded the opened area.

Around the balcony, drooping in the heat and light from the upper windows, creating an indoor garden for her apartment behind its Victorian facade, were the plants Anna had collected and nurtured since girlhood.

"They're alive," she whispered, unable to hide her surprise or her relief.

She saw Evan looking around the shop, a puzzled expression dragging his dark brows together as he examined the hasty and often crude repairs and the bare walls where once her display racks had stood.

"The accident was months ago, Anna," he said. "Why hasn't the insurance company done something about restoring this place?"

"I don't know. I had to leave most of the decisions to my sister and to Henry Johnston, my accountant. I suppose I assumed I'd have to be involved in the actual repair process."

"Which of course you couldn't be until now?"

"Right. But now I can be." Finally the happiness, the excitement, she had always expected her homecoming to bring filled her. She smiled at Evan, knowing that her happiness had to be reflected in her eyes. "Now I can be. Would you like to see my home, Evan? I can't guarantee what condition it's in, now, but I've always been more than a little proud of what I've accomplished upstairs."

And she wanted Evan to be proud of her accomplishments, too. She suspected the apartment was a mess—Lisa had never been much of a housekeeper—but it might be the only chance she had to show Evan through the spacious rooms. And this might be the only way she had of keeping him with her, for just a little while longer.

Four

Evan suspected that Anna wanted to retract her invitation the moment they stepped into her living quarters, but after a small, shocked "Oh, dear," she tried to hide her dismay the way she had downstairs.

He set her suitcase on the floor and scraped magazines and dirty dishes aside to plunk the two plants from the hospital down onto what appeared to be a vintage walnut table beneath the clutter and grime.

Anna stood just inside the door, holding her balloon bouquet, not speaking, not moving. He freed the strings of the balloons from her fingers and secured the bouquet to one of the plants. Then he guided Anna to the nearest chair—something traditional and comfortable-looking, but buried beneath a mound of laundry. He raked the clothing onto the floor and nudged Anna toward the chair.

"Sit," he commanded gently.

She sat. He suspected she would have been unable to do anything else. He watched her eyes as they focused on one area of the room, then another, and still another—each in as much disarray as the last. And he watched the emotions she would never be able completely to hide darken and shadow her eyes.

Now, defenseless as Anna was, he could almost read her thoughts. And they echoed his. Where was Lisa? She hadn't had to pick Anna up at the hospital, hadn't had to bring her home, hadn't had to put herself out in any way. But she must have known Anna was coming home, must have known what time she would be here. Why hadn't she been here to meet Anna? Evan glanced around the room again. Why had Lisa allowed Anna to see—why had she *flaunted*— how little she valued Anna's home or Anna's feelings?

Anna reached across a nearby table and moved a delicate figurine to safety, away from the edge, and then started to rise.

"Sit," Evan said again, kneeling in front of her. "I didn't know the truck had managed to climb your stairs."

She looked up at him sharply. He was smiling, and he hoped to God it was convincing. Apparently it was. He saw a corner of her lips twitch. Then a small, slightly watery chuckle broke from her.

"Do you think the insurance company will pay for the cleanup?" she asked. "It shouldn't take a competent crew more than a week or so."

Her hands still clutched the arms of the chair. He covered one with his own and felt the tension easing from her. "Good girl," he said. "Now sit here while I find your kitchen and make us some coffee."

She nodded, and he rose to his feet. "Evan," she said softly. "Be careful."

He saw the twinkle in her eyes as she pointed toward a doorway to the right. "I'm not sure it's safe in there."

Evan wasn't sure anywhere near Anna Harrison was safe for him. And he was sure it was too late to be careful. He found the kitchen at the back of the apartment. Atrium doors led from it to a small balcony and an outside stair-case. The plants there had not fared as well as the ones in-side.

Lisa had obviously been there—probably not too long before their arrival. He recognized the perfume still hang-ing in the air as one his mother frequently used. A lipstick-smeared cup balanced precariously on the edge of the sink.

He washed two cups and found a small tin of tea bags. Then, giving up on finding coffee or a kettle or a clean pan, he filled the cups with water and shoved them into the microwave.

He ought to leave, he thought as he waited for the water to boil, ought to walk out the door and forget all about Anna Harrison, her thoughtless sister, her ruined business and her desecrated home. Ought to forget how, even glazed by pain and anesthesia, her dark eyes had smiled at him. Ought to forget how slight and fragile she had felt in his arms as he held her the night her bandages came off. Ought to forget how *he* had felt that night.

Evan didn't believe in love, didn't believe in romance, in knights on white chargers, in fairy tales, in happily-ever-after. But the other night, as he held her, he'd felt like con-queror, protector, defender... and lover.

He ought to leave. Now. But Evan knew that if he left, Anna would immediately start to work, either on the apart-ment or downstairs, and she was already worn out, ex-hausted by the slight exertion of the trip home.

He'd noted the bare pantry while searching for coffee. Now he opened the refrigerator. No food. At least none he thought safe to eat.

No food, no car, no one to keep her from working her-self into some sort of relapse, and no energy to cope with what had to be done.

Leave Anna Harrison alone in that condition?

Not likely.

A blue phone hung on the wall of the once-cheerful blue, yellow and orange kitchen. Evan snatched the receiver off the hook and punched in a well-remembered series of numbers.

Tom Fairmont took his call immediately.

"I'm at Anna Harrison's apartment," Evan said tersely. "I need your help, not your arguments or your permission." In a matter of minutes, Evan had arranged for a cleanup crew, carpenters, masons, glaziers—taking care of all the things that should have been done months before but had been left for Anna to deal with.

Then he called his own home. He had little need for a housekeeper, but Jane Mudge had worked for his father years earlier, and when Evan returned from Europe she had shown up at his door and announced that she now worked for him. Evan wasn't sure just who worked for whom, but right now he knew exactly where Jane was needed.

The least cluttered place was the balcony garden overlooking Anna's shop. Evan carried their cups out there, and they sat at a plant-laden wrought-iron table, in gaily cushioned rattan chairs. Anna sat to one side, half sheltered by the lacy fronds of some type of palm, the left side of her face in shadow. He wondered if she had chosen that chair consciously or subconsciously. He wondered if she realized that now, even if there once had been, there was no reason to hide in the shadows.

Anna picked up her cup, traced its rim with her fingers and set it down again. "Evan, I . . ."

He recognized the dismissal in her voice, so at odds with the pleading in her eyes. Did she have any idea how she looked at him? He doubted it. He'd recognized a streak of pride in Anna that was as strong and true as the rest of her character, and he knew she'd be humiliated to learn that her needs and emotions were so easy to read.

He placed his hand over hers on the table, stilling her restless motions. "Yes, I do have to stay," he told her. "Yes, I *want* to stay. And, no, there is nothing else I need to be doing right now.

"Anna..." Maybe it wasn't any of his business, but this was a subject they had skirted and avoided too long. "Where is your sister?"

"I..."

He felt her hand tense under his. When it didn't relax, he squeezed it gently. He saw the glimmer of moisture in her eyes, but she blinked it away.

"I don't know, Evan. It's the middle of the morning. The shop should be open, but it's obvious it hasn't been for a long time. I don't understand what's happened here."

"Has she always lived with you?"

Anna shook her head in a quick little negative gesture. "No. Only as long as she had to. She was just fourteen when our parents died. I was twenty—the judge didn't have any problem with appointing me her guardian, but Lisa did. Uncle Toby was still alive then—he's the man who uncovered this beautiful staircase for me and did so much of the finish carpentry in my apartment.

"He helped me with Lisa, helped me to try to understand what she was going through. He died of cancer last year.

"Lisa had her own place by then, she'd moved out on her eighteenth birthday. His death really hurt her. She locked herself in her apartment for over a week, wouldn't come out, wouldn't talk to anyone. Didn't even come to the funeral. She's had so many losses.

"She's only twenty-two. Maybe I expected too much of her. But I was so happy when she offered to move in here and take care of things while I was in the hospital."

Anna looked at him, her eyes once again dark, wounded. "Why did she offer to help if she didn't intend to?"

"Did she need money?" he suggested. "A place to live?"

"I don't think so. Our parents left us a little money."
Anna shrugged. "Most of my money is tied up in this
building and my business, but Lisa gets a reasonable income from—from a trust. She already had an apartment she
seemed quite satisfied with, so I couldn't have given her
anything she didn't already have."

Except access to your inventory and your cashbox, Evan
thought. But he didn't say it. He couldn't say it. Because
that was a realization Anna would have to come to on her
own. And, if true, it might just complete the destruction his
family's truck had started.

He hoped he was wrong. He hoped Anna's sister was
anything but the greedy, conniving, totally self-centered
person her actions indicated. Anna excused Lisa's behavior
because of the losses she'd suffered. But what about Anna's
losses? She'd come through the same ones—and more.

Jane Mudge arrived with groceries and a packed picnic
basket less than two hours after Evan called her. She banished Evan and Anna to the balcony garden while she muttered about fragile cups and quiet places.

Anna protested, as Evan had known she would, and Jane
relentlessly persisted, as he'd known *she* would. But the
lunch revived Anna, and afterward she resumed the only
task he had allowed her to start before Jane's arrival: watering her drooping garden.

"I should be helping her," Anna said, looking toward her
apartment for perhaps the dozenth time. "I shouldn't let her
clean that mess all by herself."

Evan took the watering can from her and set it in the tub
of a large, bushy-leafed plant. Shaking his head, he fought
the laughter he felt building within him. *Laughter?* Not for
years had he felt the sheer joy, the luxury, of laughter.

"Listen to me," he said sternly. "Nobody *lets* Jane
Mudge do *anything.* Didn't you notice? She took charge the
moment she got here, and neither one of us will be able to

stop her from doing what she thinks is necessary. But she's not here to clean your home, Anna, just to supervise the cleaning crew that's on the way."

"A cleaning crew?"

"And carpenters. Jane will take the pressure of supervision and free you for what's really important to you—your clay, I think—and let you get some rest when you need to. All right?"

For a moment, he thought she was going to argue. For a moment, she looked at him through clouded and questioning eyes. Then the barest ghost of a smile softened her lips and chased the clouds from her eyes. She lifted her hands to his face and held them against his cheeks, touching him as he had touched her at the hospital.

"I don't know why you're doing this," she said, leaning forward and brushing her lips against his cheek, "but thank you. I think this is one of the nicest things anyone has ever done for me."

Anna had visited her workroom, but the arrival of the carpenters had driven her from there. She had attempted to help Jane, but the arrival of the cleaning crew had effectively banished her from her apartment. Now she sat at the wrought-iron table on the balcony, catalogues and order forms spread around her, with concentration distorting the perfect symmetry of her face as she looked down over her empty shelves and display cabinets.

And now Evan felt chased away. He wandered into the kitchen, which was not yet sparkling but was rapidly being made that way, and where Jane Mudge temporarily reigned in isolation. She had taken over the task of cleaning and protecting Anna's fragile breakables, and she stood in front of the sink, hands plunged in soapy water, when Evan entered the room.

Jane turned toward him as he entered the kitchen. She didn't actually grin—Jane seldom loosened up quite that much—but he heard droll amusement in her voice when she said, "I once worked for a family with two sons in college. The family had bought a house for them to live in—some sort of tax advantage, I believe—and for Christmas one year they gave the boys a week of my services. That place was worse than this one, I think. Of course, they had probably had a year longer to get it in that condition."

"Did you work for that family much longer?" Evan asked, for the moment willing to play straight man for Jane's skewed sense of humor.

"No."

"Does this mean you're going to free me from your services anytime soon?"

Jane shook her head. One iron gray curl worked loose from the bun at her nape. With soapy fingers, she tucked it back in. "Not on a bet. I thought you were scheduled for terminal boredom until you shared this interesting facet of your life with me. There may be hope for the boy I once knew after all."

A horn sounded, loud and angry even over the hammering of the carpenters below, the powerful hum of a vacuum somewhere in the apartment and the *whoosh, gurgle* and *thunk* of the washer and dryer.

Evan walked to the atrium doors, now opened so that the numerous ceiling fans throughout the building could draw in fresh air, and looked down over the small parking area behind the building.

A fire-engine red import he didn't recognize from this angle, its sunroof open, had pulled in from the alley. Now it worked its way around the various pickup trucks and vans littering the area and squeezed into a space next to his company-leased Chevrolet.

A tall, leggy blonde dressed in very short shorts and a torso-hugging halter stepped from the car, tossed her permed—and probably skillfully tinted—curls back from her face and stood glaring at the parking lot.

Jane wiped her hands on a dish towel and walked to Evan's side. "Who is that?" she asked.

Evan grimaced. If not for Anna's tender emotions, he might have found the confrontation he sensed was coming amusing, might have enjoyed treating that young woman to the kind of chastisement she deserved. Instead, he would have to control himself. Lisa was Anna's problem, not his. "If I'm not mistaken," he told Jane, "this *facet* of my life just got a little more interesting."

Evan and Anna had come through the back door and up the front stairs. Since then, he had noticed a narrower staircase leading down into the storeroom. He didn't know which entrance Anna's sister would choose, but, for some reason he didn't explore, Evan found it important to speak with Lisa before she encountered Anna.

The outside stairs were more of a fire escape than anything else, but since the doors were unlocked and open, they were usable.

Evan stepped out onto the rear balcony and to the railing. "Miss Harrison?" he called down to the young woman. "Lisa?"

The woman looked up at him, and the scowl on her face transformed itself into a practiced, provocative smile. If Evan hadn't seen that same smile so often—on his mother's face as she went after a new conquest, on the face of his fiancée when she hadn't yet given up hope of reeling him in, on the faces of numerous acquaintances and wives of friends in the circle of people he couldn't seem to escape—he might have believed it genuine.

She was always the pretty one, he thought as Lisa lithely navigated her way up the old iron staircase. Her features didn't have the delicacy or the bone-deep beauty of Anna's, but they did have a type of beauty many women would willingly go under the scalpel to achieve.

And they had never been marred by scar tissue or discolored flesh.

Was that how it had been for Anna? Forever in the shadow of her *pretty* sister? Or was Evan only projecting onto a healthy, happy family what he thought might have happened?

Lisa reached the top of the stairs, and Evan opened the small gate in the railing to allow her to enter. She wasn't quite as tall as Anna; her figure was a little fuller. And she was appraising him as carefully, and apparently as casually, as he was appraising her.

"Are you with the insurance company?"

Evan heard Jane cough once as she moved back toward the sink.

"I'm here as a result of the accident," he said.

Lisa went into the kitchen, glanced at Jane and turned to face Evan. "Good. I see Anna found someone. You have no idea how hard it is to hire competent domestic help these days."

She dug in the envelope bag she carried and found a pen and a cash-register receipt. "This is my new address and phone number," she told him, writing as she spoke. "I know you'll want to talk to me about the accident, the property loss. Things like that," she added, looking at him from beneath coyly lowered lashes.

This barracuda was still in the baby stage, Evan thought, willing to sharpen her teeth on another victim, but not yet as skillful in the hunt as she thought she was.

Lisa waved a hand in the direction of the vehicles in the parking lot. "I see she also didn't waste any time in getting the repairs started once *she* had to live in this bombed-out relic. Of course, Anna always has been the self-sufficient one."

She handed him the slip of paper. "Call me anytime. I'd be happy to talk, but now I've got to get some things together to take over to my new place."

Even as accustomed as he was to manipulation and self-ishness on a level this child would probably never manage to achieve, Evan was shocked by Lisa's callousness.

"You're leaving? The day your sister gets home from the hospital, you're going to move out?"

"So?" The mask of sophistication slipped just a little, allowing him a glimpse of the girl Lisa might be hiding, then was pushed firmly back in place "Now that Anna's home, there's no need for me to stay.

"Besides, I have an active social life. You've seen Anna. You can understand why I wouldn't want to expose a date to her... to her... well, to the way she looks."

Anna hadn't told her. It had been days since her bandages were removed. Why hadn't she told her own sister about the surgery that had been so important to her? Lack of opportunity? Or an unwillingness to expose her new hopes and dreams to someone who wouldn't care? *Oh, Anna*, he thought. *Have you ever had anyone who really cared?*

Glancing over Lisa's shoulder, Evan caught sight of Jane glaring at the young woman's back. Jane's expression spoke eloquently of the harsh words she kept locked inside.

Evan lifted one brow in silent, shared acknowledgment of Jane's anger, before finding words for Lisa. "Yes," he said quietly. "I certainly can understand your reluctance to expose your dates to your sister. But now, why don't we go find her? I know she's been looking forward to seeing you."

Anna lifted her head from the order forms, rubbed her temples and then massaged the back of her neck. Her checkbook lay open to one side of her, her general account book across the table.

Her business was in worse shape than she had ever imagined. But if she cut back on the amount of inventory she normally carried, if she arranged her displays carefully, so that no one would notice, if she worked at her wheel as if the wolf were at the door, she might just make it.

She lifted her cup and took a sip of now-cool tea before she realized that Evan was no longer hovering nearby. Evan had been a godsend today. There was no way she could have gotten any of the work done that he accomplished with no apparent effort. But even if he hadn't taken charge, his companionship would have gotten her through this day, if her pride hadn't attempted to chase him out the door the minute he brought her home. Thank God he hadn't let her do that.

Anna smiled at the thought of even trying to chase Evan away from something he had set his mind on. She couldn't imagine ever being able to do that. Her smile slipped a little. She also couldn't imagine why he had taken such an interest in her or her business. Unless that interest was prompted by guilt.

Ridiculous, Anna thought. Evan had had nothing to do with the accident. He hadn't even been in the country. And therefore had no control over the company that owned the truck that had hit her. He hadn't even known about the accident until she had been well on the way to recovery.

Almost without thought, in an action born of long habit, Anna's hand lifted and cradled her cheek, covering the smooth, tender skin that was no longer marred by her birthmark. *Could he be prompted by guilt?*

And, if not guilt, what? Could it truly be that Evan was interested in her, Anna Harrison, as a woman?

Her hand still in place, Anna shook her head. No man had ever been interested in her and only one had ever pretended to be. She let her fingers caress her cheek.

She hadn't tried her new appearance out in public yet, only in the safety of the hospital, and here, with the work crews, but she had seen the difference in the way people looked at her. Not one of the workmen had averted his eyes or invented an excuse to make a hasty retreat from her. No one had stared at her surreptitiously with aversion or fear or disgust. However, she had caught one man staring with what she thought might be appreciation. Even a little lust, maybe? And that had been a truly novel feeling for her.

She leaned back in her chair, easing her shoulders but still cupping her cheek, as she looked through the fronds of a large areca palm over the railing and down into the showroom. She could worry about how her new appearance affected people later. She could, and probably would, worry about Evan's motivations later. Right now, she needed to be concerned about her business and, more importantly, her sister.

And these two concerns seemed irrevocably linked. She hadn't seen or heard from Lisa in days. She should have been prepared for this disaster. At the time of their last conversation, Lisa had all but warned her. *I don't have a head for business,* Lisa had insisted then, but not until then. *I never have. You know that, Anna. You've got to get home and take care of things. It's more than I can handle. It's more than you can expect me to handle.*

Why hadn't Lisa said anything before then? And why hadn't Henry Johnston warned her in one of her many telephone calls to him? Surely he'd known something was wrong when he prepared her taxes, her quarterly statements, all the reports he insisted were so necessary. Hadn't he? But he'd simply told her that although things could be better, she should spend her energy on her recovery and not worry about a business she could do nothing about from a hospital bed. But surely she could have done *something.*

And Lisa? What had happened to Lisa? She refused to believe that her own sister could be as uncaring as she had seemed these past few months. Something had to be seriously wrong in Lisa's life.

She heard the sound of approaching voices and looked up to see the two persons most in her thoughts walk out onto the balcony from the apartment. Lisa was smiling up at

Evan, smiling that magical smile that had had her parents, all the aunts and uncles, all the teachers, even the few boys Anna had once let herself dream about before she finally realized the futility of it, hurrying to do anything she wanted.

Not him! Anna thought as a sharp, brutal pain clutched her heart. *You can't have him, too!*

And then Anna banished that thought, though the pain lingered. Evan wasn't hers to keep or give away.

Lisa looked at her then, and Anna recognized the expression on her sister's face, the one that said, *I've got a really good excuse for what's happened, and none of it's my fault.*

Regardless, she found a smile for Lisa, then remembered that she was still cupping her cheek. She lowered her hand and started to rise, to go to her sister and hug her.

Lisa's eyes widened. Her mouth opened soundlessly before she found words. "Your *face!* My God!" she said, lifting her hand to her mouth. "What have you done to your face?"

Five

Anna turned and stretched in bed. Her own bed, at last. The linens were clean and fresh and smelled of sunshine. The entire apartment carried the aromas of lemon oil, carpet freshener and good, clean summer air. Coming through the open windows of her bedroom, the air was still cool, still slightly moist, but not oppressive, and for this brief moment free of the intrusive odors of traffic.

The sky was still shaded with the unfulfilled promise of morning. The birds knew morning approached, though. Three doors down, a building had a small roof garden, and next door to that the owners had dug up a portion of their rear parking area and built a courtyard with grass, with trees. The birds had found those places, as well as Anna's own feeders and waterers, which she had replenished yesterday, and now they chattered noisily, happily, as they welcomed morning.

Anna wasn't sure she welcomed the beginning of a new day. Yesterday had been too full of unwelcome, unwanted revelations.

Her sister desperately needed help. Her business desperately needed her attention. And sometime during the innocent card games, her private and unvoiced teasing about healthy lust, the building of what she had convinced herself was just friendship, she had fallen hopelessly in love with Evan Claymore.

She *ached.* Her eyes ached from the pressure of unshed tears, her heart ached from futile longing, her body ached from too-long-denied needs.

All her life, Anna had faced her challenges head-on, defying them to do their worst. Now, maybe they had. Maybe this would be the time when she couldn't go on, couldn't smile, couldn't accept what fate handed out, couldn't begin again.

What she wanted most of all was to pull the clean, fresh sheets up over her head and hide there in her bed.

But she couldn't do that.

She wasn't alone in the apartment.

Lisa had left, almost immediately, wounded, hurt, betrayed, by Anna's not having told her about her face. *When, Lisa? When could I have told you? Where were you when I needed to tell you?*

Evan had left, too, almost reluctantly, after Anna convinced him she wouldn't be able to do any of the things she had to do as long as he remained.

Jane Mudge had simply refused to leave. "You convinced that boy you're all right," she had said, "but I know better. I took myself on a little shopping trip up the street when I saw how things were going around here. I have everything I need for the night, so don't think you're going to get rid of me, too."

Anna had responded by taking a large mug of tea and closing herself in her bedroom. Now Jane slept somewhere in the apartment, and in a few hours workmen would again be crawling all over the place.

In the meantime, though, even if Anna couldn't pull the covers over her head, there was something she could do. She slipped out of bed and threw on old jeans and a T-shirt and crept quietly out of her room and down the stairs.

Very little had been done in her workroom so far. Anna hesitated at the door and then decided to ignore the mess. There would be plenty of time later for cleaning, even for creating pots and vases and dishes, plenty of time for the clay and all the healing it could bring her. Now she needed a different kind of healing.

She stored her wax in a closed cabinet against a wall that was actually below ground level on this hillside street. Miraculously, the wax was perfectly intact. Anna took it, and the fitted case of tools she stored with it, to her worktable. She pushed the clutter to one side and tossed a drape over the table before setting the wax down.

At one time she'd thought she would sculpt Evan in bronze, if she ever did him. Would she do his likeness now? It didn't matter. She had brought so much beauty into her life with her skill; whatever she found in the wax today could only be healing. Smiling slightly, already lost in the creative process, she dragged a chair to her table and began to search the wax for its secret forms.

"What do you want from her?"

Evan took the tall glass of iced tea Jane thrust at him and leaned back against Anna's now-gleaming kitchen counter. "What do you mean?"

"I mean, Evan Claymore, what's your interest in this young woman? Why are you spending so much time with her? In short, what do you want from her?"

Evan took a long drink from the glass, debating what he would answer, if anything at all. The words were couched differently, but they were essentially the same words Bill

Hatfield had asked him when he inquired about Anna's surgery. What *did* he want from her? He wasn't any more sure of his answer than when Bill had asked. And why were these two people so certain he wanted anything?

"Is it inconceivable that I just want friendship?" he asked.

"With a woman, Evan? Won't that be a first for you?"

Now an unexpected flare of anger sharpened Evan's words. "You walked out of my life years ago. How do you know what will or won't be a first for me? And what makes you think you have the right to ask?"

Jane shook her head, ignoring all but his last question. "You gave me the right when you asked me to take care of that child. And she is a child, Evan, in her experience. But in no other way. She's a woman, with the needs of a woman. Needs that you have enough knowledge and skill to take advantage of. So if all you intend to do is play with her a little while, satisfy some physical needs of your own and maybe assuage a little guilt, back off, before you do her serious damage."

"I don't intend to hurt her, Jane."

Jane pondered his quietly spoken words for a moment before finally nodding her head. "I'm staying here, you know," she told him. "At least for the next week or so. Until Anna gets her shop open. Until she resolves some of the problems with that sister of hers."

"What did Anna say about that?"

Jane took the barely touched glass from him, refilled it and handed it back to him. "I haven't told her yet."

Evan felt a smile building. Anna wouldn't stand a chance against Jane's determination. Just as quickly as it came, his smile faded. Would Anna stand a chance against his?

Nonsense, he told himself. He wouldn't hurt Anna. He valued her friendship, her smile, her good opinion of him, too much to jeopardize them. As for the physical needs Jane had challenged him on, he hadn't even known what Anna looked like until a few days ago. Well, maybe he *had* fantasized about the woman behind the bandages. Maybe he *had* wondered about the slender figure in the shapeless hospital gowns. Maybe more than one dream about a fascinating and mysterious woman *had* awakened him and left him frustrated and sleepless. But Anna wasn't the mysterious woman his dreams made her. She was open and honest and guileless and—and every bit as alluring and fascinating as the woman in his dreams.

"Where is she?" he asked. "Resting?"

"She's working," Jane told him. "Since early this morning. And don't you bother her," she said as Evan turned toward the stairwell. "She's got something more than sculpture to work on today."

Anna slowly became aware of the muted sounds of workmen in the building outside her closed studio. Sighing, stretching, she pushed back from her worktable and studied the wax figure nested among her tools. No, she hadn't captured Evan, not even in wax, but she might have found herself.

She was quite sure the sculpture wasn't biologically correct; a less-than-critical examination would show that the work wasn't meant to be realistic. Nor was it truly abstract.

Anna had worked through many counseling sessions following the accident. She wondered what her counselor would think of this.

This figure would hang from a metal branch, which Anna would prepare later. It was fairly small compared to work she had previously done, but proportionately slender—a cocoon, and emerging from it, one wing completely free and beginning to spread, and another just fighting its way free. A butterfly. This would be a monochrome in bronze, its color provided only by the shading and shadows of the detailing Anna would carefully work into its texture.

She heard a knock on the door and turned, curious. She didn't remember having closed the door. The door opened, and Evan stepped into her workroom. He looked at her and then at her work, almost solemnly, in a way she had never seen before. In an ingrained defensive gesture she no longer questioned, Anna tossed a drape over her work. She started to smooth her shirt, but then thought better of it and stilled her hand. She was working, after all. And the wax had left her cleaner than the clay usually did. Did her appearance offend Evan? Was that why he was looking at her so strangely?

"I have orders not to disturb you," he said, smiling at last. "But I thought you might be hungry."

Anna straightened the tools on her bench, gathering her thoughts as she did so, bringing herself back to the conscious world from the realm of imagination and freedom. Maybe Evan's words explained his strange attitude. Surely no one but Jane, or perhaps Eileen Claymore, would presume to give this man orders.

"I am hungry," she admitted, only now realizing she was. "I suppose I missed breakfast."

He nodded. "And lunch." He took a step closer to her table. "You must have really been engrossed in your work. May I see?"

"No." Her denial was instinctive, born of early rejection and ridicule and having no basis in the acceptance her work now received, no basis in anything Evan had ever said or done to make her think he wouldn't value her work.

She sighed and shook her head. "Habit," she said. She lifted the drape. "Of course you may look."

He didn't lift the work from the table; he seemed almost afraid to touch it. But finally he did extend his hand. With gentle fingers, he reached out and traced a delicate pattern across the butterfly's spreading wing.

Anna realized she was holding her breath. She was able to release her breath, but not to draw her mesmerized eyes away from the sight of Evan caressing something that only moments ago she had compared to herself. His touch was so light, so hesitant, that it would not have injured a living butterfly. Was that how he would touch her—*if* he touched her?

Carefully Evan drew his hand away from her work and turned to face her, studying her with the same intensity with which he had just studied the wax figure. "You are . . . unbelievably talented," he said quietly.

Anna grew uneasy under his scrutiny. Few persons had ever looked at her directly before. And she knew how she must look. She had paid no heed to the dust that covered the room, and now it covered her. Her feet were bare and cold against the concrete floor. Her cheek, though no longer scarred, still bore the last traces of her surgery.

Restless, she ran her fingers through her short, spiky hair. She laughed shakily, trying to dispel the tension she felt. It didn't work. "And unbelievably messy," she said.

"Don't."

Evan's hands captured hers as they speared through her hair, stilling them, stilling her. "Don't ever put yourself down again," he said.

His hands dropped to her shoulders, and she knew he had to feel the tension in her; she felt it mirrored in his touch.

"Come here, Anna," he said softly. "Just let me hold you. I know it's been a hell of a homecoming for you."

She ought to protest, but she didn't—she couldn't. Instead, she went into his arms as though she belonged there. She felt his slight hesitation as her breast brushed his chest, as her cheek settled against his throat. Then his arms drew her closer, nestling her against him, wrapping her in the warmth of him, the comfort of him that for only a moment was comfort to her. That for only a moment was comfort to him.

She felt the change in the cadence of his heartbeat, felt the tremor in his arms as they tightened around her. "Oh, God," she heard him whisper. "It's true."

"Evan?"

"Sshh," he murmured, "it's all right. I promise. I'll make it all right." Then he began releasing her slowly, releasing her as cautiously as he had held her.

"Evan?" she said again, not knowing what she asked, not knowing if she wanted an answer.

He stepped away from her and dropped his hands to his sides. "Do you need to put your work away before we go to lunch?"

She nodded.

"Do you need any help?"

"No," she said. With hands that trembled only slightly, she placed work and tools on a waiting tray and tucked it in the cabinet. What was true? And what was so wrong that Evan had to promise to make it right? she wondered.

"Ready?" he asked.

Maybe, she thought as she rose from kneeling before the cabinet. But she wanted to cry, *Ready for what? What's happening, Evan? Why did you hold me? Why did you let me go? And what do those words you probably don't realize you spoke aloud mean?*

"Yes," she said, finding a smile and firmly fixing it in place as she turned to face him. "Yes, I am."

The next morning, the air in her room was already heated, still and oppressive when Anna awoke. She stretched, dislodging the sheet she had already partially kicked away, and felt what seemed like every muscle in her body protest. She didn't think she'd done so much in the past two days that she'd abused her body, but apparently she had. "Damn," she muttered softly. "When am I going to be over this?"

She showered in the light and spacious bathroom adjoining her bedroom, sluicing away the last of the fog clouding her sleep-drugged mind, sluicing away a few of her aches and some of her unexpected reluctance to begin a new day.

She hesitated a few moments longer in the bathroom, admiring the now-gleaming white porcelain fixtures, the tiny, spotless white ceramic tiles on the floor, the white marble windowsills beneath frosted glass. She'd wrapped herself in an emerald green bath sheet and she stood on an oversize coordinated rug, both of which smelled impossibly of sunshine and fresh-mown grass.

Evan had done this for her, Anna thought as she looked around the room. Without his thoughtfulness, this would still be a dingy gray, or she would be on her hands and knees scrubbing it.

Anna lifted the edge of the bath sheet to her face and breathed deeply of its inviting aroma. The workmen had scrubbed the tiles and fixtures, she knew, but Jane had to be responsible for the laundry. Jane, who had taken it upon herself to become a combination mother hen and drill sergeant to Anna, who even now, if Anna properly identified the faint noises coming from her bedroom, was in the next room, picking up after her. Sighing, Anna slipped into a robe and reached for the doorknob. She didn't need anyone picking up after her, no matter how well-intentioned that someone was.

Jane looked up from smoothing the last pillow in its sham over the now neatly spread comforter. "I love these old beds," Jane said, smiling. "But where did you find a dust ruffle with a long enough drop? That's always seemed to me to be the one problem. That and…well, you're tall enough so you don't need a step to get in it."

Anna shook her head, smiling, as she entered the bedroom. "Thank you for making the bed, but you don't have to clean up my messes, you know."

Jane smiled at her. "I know I don't have to. And that's precisely why I don't mind." Her smile faded as she studied Anna. "A little sore, are you, today? I thought you were overdoing it yesterday, but I also thought you wouldn't appreciate anyone telling you so."

Anna felt a reluctant chuckle building, and gave it its freedom. Maybe this day wouldn't be so bad after all.

"That's more like it," Jane said. Abruptly she turned and marched across the room, pausing and looking back just before she closed the door behind her. "Breakfast will be ready in ten minutes."

She didn't wait long enough for Anna to protest, and Anna realized she really didn't want to protest. She was hungry—for food and for the low-key pampering Jane insisted on giving her. Jane would be gone soon, and then it would be back to business as usual, but for now, what could it hurt for Anna to accept something that seemed so freely given?

Anna found breakfast waiting for her on the small table just outside the atrium doors of the kitchen: a fresh fruit compote, croissants from the bakery a few doors up the street, milk that appeared to have much more butterfat than the two percent she usually allowed herself, and small containers of whipped butter, cream cheese and strawberry preserves, all served on the pretty little breakfast dishes Anna had collected years ago and now never seemed to find the time to use.

She seated herself at the table and picked up the waiting napkin—one of the set she had once made to go with these dishes—and looked at the tempting array of food. "Are you trying to fatten me up?"

Jane brought a pot of coffee to the table and sat down across from Anna, pouring each of them a cup. "As a matter of fact, I am. Now eat," she said gently.

Anna did just that, surprising herself by enjoying the meal as though she hadn't had decent food in months. Finally, though, she had to sigh, sit back and push the last, still-tempting croissant across the table toward Jane, out of easy reach.

"That was so good, Jane," she said, knowing it was time she released Jane, but strangely reluctant to do so. "I don't know if I can ever tell you how much I appreciate what you've done for me, but you must have better things to do with your time than baby-sit a stranger."

Jane shook her head. "No, I don't. I have Evan's house almost in order. What remains to be done, I can do from here." She smiled. It was a strange little smile that Anna found odd and almost disconcerting. "In fact, I can probably do it much better from here."

"I don't understand," Anna said.

"You don't have to, dear." Jane patted her hand, then rose and began briskly clearing the table. "Evan wants to go with you this afternoon to begin shopping for a replacement for your van. Before then, though, you have another appointment." Jane put the few dishes she carried on the counter and reached for a ring of keys waiting there. "Take my car," she said. "Your appointment is in Fort Smith in an hour, so you don't have time to do much more than dress before you have to leave."

Did anyone ever win an argument with Jane Mudge, Anna wondered later that morning. Surely someone had at some time. About *something*. But Anna wasn't that person, and she hadn't found the time or the topic. She'd heard of the salon where she now sat in regal, if somewhat odd, splendor, compliments of Jane's benevolent manipulation; a few of her more affluent patrons had mentioned it. But Anna had never dreamed she would be the center of attention in any establishment quite so... so decadent.

She had been creamed and patted and shampooed and trimmed and dried and examined, and then the mirrors had been taken away. "I'll teach you how to do this later," an intense young man told her as he spread an array of pots and tubes and vials and brushes and styling dryers on the table beside her, "but first I want you to have the full effect of it without concern for technique."

The full effect was breathtaking. Anna sat silently for several moments, just staring at the stranger in the mirror who stared back at her. Then, rising, she turned and walked to the larger mirrors at the stylist's workstation. The face she saw was hers, yet, curiously, not *her*. She raised a trembling hand to her left cheek. Even the slight redness was gone, hidden by makeup so skillfully applied that she appeared to be wearing none. Her cheekbones, enhanced by her weight loss, were now subtly emphasized; her eyes seemed enormous, dark, mysterious, framed by sooty lashes; her mouth, soft, vulnerable. Her hair, though still short, now seemed modishly styled instead of punk-rock spiky.

If Anna hadn't already shed more tears than she'd ever thought she possessed, she would have cried then. Who was this elegant woman who studied her with as much intense scrutiny as she studied her? Was it possible that *she* could be Anna Harrison?

Evan knew he was overstepping the bounds for a disinterested party by taking Anna shopping for a new vehicle. And he knew with equal certainty that he was going to do it anyway. He knew any number of people who would say he was trying to ensure his place in Anna's good graces so that she wouldn't deal Riverland its deathblow. He knew some who would say his motives were even more base than that. Few would believe his real reason. He wasn't even sure he believed it, himself.

He wasn't tying Anna to him by obligation; he was freeing her. Freeing her so that if she turned to him, he'd know it was because she wanted to, not because she had no other options. A new vehicle—or so he'd convinced himself—was a necessary step in her path to that freedom.

He pulled his own car into the loading zone in front of her shop and sat looking at the transformation taking place. Fortunately, the structural damage had been slight, although quite a bit of the brick needed replacing, as well as most of the wood trim and all of the glass. Evan closed his eyes against too-vivid pictures. Another foot or so in either direction, and the truck would have either missed Anna's van altogether . . . or trapped her in the resulting fire.

Idiot! His eyes snapped open. When he'd brought Anna home from the hospital, he'd blithely parked in the same spot. *Is something wrong?* he'd asked her then. He hadn't been completely insensitive; he'd noticed her distress. He just hadn't had the sense to realize she must be reliving the last time she had been parked in that spot. And she'd smiled at him and tried to put him at ease!

"Damn it, Anna," he muttered as he put the car in gear and eased into traffic and headed for the cross street that led to the alley behind her shop. "You're going to have to learn not to let people walk all over your emotions."

His mood hadn't improved by the time he found a parking place in the back alley. He looked up at the balcony. The gate in the railing was closed; for some reason, so were the doors leading out onto the balcony. The double doors to her small loading platform stood open, apparently for the benefit of the high-sided trailer backed up to it. As he watched, two men came out the door, lugging a tarp loaded with broken pieces of drywall, glass and lumber, and dumped the contents into the trailer.

Evan nodded at the men as he passed them, glanced into the closed-off, dark and empty workroom and made his way through the building to the front stairs, past the sights and sounds and smells of destruction and construction existing together in some crazy hodgepodge of creativity. Yesterday the dust had been pervasive, existing, growing, but not truly aggressive. Today it smothered everything, nearly obliterating the dark gleam of walnut on the stairway; it rose in the air, dancing in the hot shafts of sunlight pouring in from the upper windows, and then fell to cover anything in its path.

He mounted the stairs quickly, but stopped when he reached the closed door of Anna's apartment. Yesterday and the day before he had entered her private rooms freely and wandered through them at will. But yesterday Jane had admitted him to the apartment, and the day before Anna had invited him in.

A small brass bell, suspended by an ornate twining bracket and surmounted by an equally ornate brass angel, hung on the facing beside the door. Evan grinned. He didn't know how anyone would be able to hear one small bell over the cacophony of noises rising from the shop below, but he pulled on the bell chain and waited.

Jane opened the front door in a matter of moments, almost as though she had been waiting for his arrival, admitting him into the peaceful oasis of Anna's living quarters. A small air conditioner hummed in a window, filtering out the dust-laden air, filtering out the noises from below.

"Is Anna ready?" he asked.

"Oh, yes." Jane smiled an odd little smile he didn't remember seeing before. But then, his memories of Jane Mudge had a sizable gap in them.

"Jane, is that—"

Anna entered the living room from the hallway, pausing just inside the room, and Evan felt as though one of those workmen below had just sawed the floor out from under his feet.

She wore a cream-colored silk dress, patterned with greens and golds and rusts. The silk draped over her breasts, kissing them, caressing them, and hugged her waist gently before sliding over her hips to swirl around her long, graceful legs. The silk dress, and the graceful high-heeled sandals that showcased her slender ankles, made her legs look as though they went on forever.

She looked at him hesitantly, as though waiting for him to judge her appearance. Dimly he was aware that she was Anna; she was the same woman he had seen yesterday in clay-stained work clothes, the same woman he had seen countless times in hospital clothes and bandages. Dimly he was aware that the changes he saw in her couldn't go deeper than makeup and an expensive hairstyle. She had been beautiful before, in a manner completely innocent and without artifice. The woman he now faced possessed a beauty his mother and countless other women he had known over the years would kill—probably quite literally—to attain.

"Anna?" he said. He wanted to say more but he wasn't sure he could speak. And he had no idea where his next words came from. "Is that you?"

She shook her head, laughed—it was a shy, defensive and somehow self-deprecating laugh—and raised her hand to her cheek in a gesture he had seen innumerable times. "I'm not sure," she said softly, shaking her head again as her eyes pleaded with him. For reassurance? This woman would never need reassurance. But Anna would, he realized as she spoke again. Softly. Hesitantly. "I'm really not sure."

Six

Anna sank back against the seat of the sedan, determined to remain quiet until Evan had guided them out of the quaint but crowded downtown area of Van Buren. The Chevrolet sedan Evan drove was comfortable enough, powerful enough for the kind of driving most people did, even attractive enough, she supposed, but it didn't match her concept of what Evan Claymore would choose for himself.

And he hadn't chosen it. He had told her the day he brought her home that the Chevrolet was a Riverland company car. The car did match her concept of what a company would choose for its employees. Staid. Attractive without being flashy. Dependable.

As for her own list of needs for a new vehicle, Anna had one primary requirement: It had to be utilitarian. And that, unbelievably, was what they were arguing about.

Evan turned onto a cross street, heading in the general direction of the interstate highway, pulled the car to the curb and turned in the seat to face her.

"You need something easier to manage than a commercial van," he said, continuing with almost the same words he had uttered before their temporary silence. "Something you can navigate in and out of tight spots, something with some pickup and power that can give you that extra burst of speed you might need to get you out of a really bad situation."

"Something like Lisa's sports car?" she asked, afraid she knew where this conversation was going. The women in Evan Claymore's life didn't drive commercial trucks. But she wasn't one of the women in his life. She was just Anna. In spite of her new disguise. And she couldn't let him make her forget that.

But he smiled at her suggestion and actually nodded his head. "Yes. Something like your sister's sports car."

"A car like that would get me killed, Evan."

"Well, maybe something a little more substantial than the tin can she drives. Maybe a small Mercedes. You know, they're really well-built vehicles, get great mileage, look good—"

"Evan!" She practically wailed his name as she reached for him, grasping his shoulders with her hands. "I'm a potter. I need a truck, not a chariot."

She felt him tense beneath her touch—the tension carried into his jaw, into his eyes, into the look that speared through her. "You're a beautiful woman, Anna. How long are you going to be satisfied with a truck?"

Uh-oh, she thought. *There's a lot more going on here than my choice of a vehicle.*

His eyes, his voice, even his question, all could have seemed cold, had she not felt the warmth, the heat, pouring from his body. What had she blundered into? And how could she blunder out of it without sacrificing her integrity? Or his?

She forced herself to look away from Evan's eyes; she knew she'd only lose herself there. Her glance fell on her hands—her hands, and yet not her hands, the hands of the woman she had met that day in the mirror.

Strangely loath to relinquish the warmth of him, she forced herself to pull her hands away, forced herself to turn slightly, forced herself to find a lightness for her voice that she didn't feel. She held her hands out for her inspection, and his.

"Do you like my manicure?"

"What?"

"I've never had one before, you know." She sighed, stretching her fingers, flexing her hands to better display them. "My nails are longer than I've ever been able to grow them before, and I believe there must be as many coats of enamel on them as that Mercedes you just tried to sell me."

"Anna, what are you talking about?"

"Cars, Evan. Vehicles, appearances, and needs. I love the way my hands look today—pampered and beautiful. I even love the way it makes me feel to look at them. Because it makes *me* feel pampered and beautiful, too.

"But what happens when I start back to work? I'll get clay under my nails immediately. I'll chip the polish. If I don't cut them, I'll break them, because they're much too long for the kind of work I have to do.

"So what do I do? Do I sacrifice these nails for the work I love? Or do I sacrifice the work I love, and who I am, in order to keep my hands looking like I've never had to work? To keep my hands looking like those of a stranger?"

Evan took her hands in his, turned them over and studied her palms and fingers. The months of enforced inactivity had softened Anna's hands, but she knew that within days she would begin rebuilding the calluses that still had not completely faded, begin replacing the nicks and cuts and bruises that she always carried.

Silently he folded her fingers into her palms and held her hands, heels and knuckles together, in his as he studied them, as he studied her. She felt the tension back in his body, but it was different somehow. This tension didn't push her away; it beckoned her.

"Maybe we can find a compromise," he said softly.

She felt tightly held breath *whoosh* out of her, felt her smile struggling to break free. "Maybe we can," she admitted softly.

The compromise they found that day was a minivan, dark green with a camel-colored interior. The customization she needed for the cargo area could be completed within two weeks, and a rental could be made road-ready and delivered to her shop the next day.

To celebrate, Evan suggested dinner and took her to a popular seafood restaurant. Anna had been there numerous times but had always requested a table in one of their private dining cubicles. That evening, they sat in the main dining room, in full sight of God and half of Fort Smith, against glass walls that overlooked the panorama of the Arkansas River and the opposite, Van Buren, side of the riverbank.

She had noticed heads turning their direction as they were escorted across the dining room to their table, had noticed the furtive admiring glances a number of the women gave Evan, and now noticed that the looks and speculation hadn't ceased.

"Do you know everyone in Fort Smith?" she asked him softly.

"Of course not," he answered, putting down his menu.

"Then why is everyone staring at you?" she asked.

Evan glanced around and then smiled at her. It was a lazy, seductive smile that held warmth and humor and a shy delight that seemed so at odds with the sophisticated appearance that Anna thought she would never grow accustomed to.

"It's not that they recognize me, Anna," he said, "they're looking at you."

She had her hand to her cheek before she realized she had moved—old fears, old insecurities, old taunts tearing through her memory and through her heart.

"Damn!" Evan muttered, reaching for her hand, lowering it to the table and holding it there. "You don't have to do that. Not ever again. These people are wondering who that beautiful woman is, and maybe, on some peripheral thought, who that very lucky man with her might be. They're wondering why they never saw you before. The men are wondering how they can meet you. The women are probably wondering how they can keep their men *from* meeting you."

Anna breathed deeply once, easing the tightness that gripped her whole body, and turned her hand under Evan's, clasping his fingers lightly. "Thank you," she said.

"For what? For telling you the truth?"

She shook her head. "For almost making me believe it. For reminding me that my life has taken a new turn, and that my old habits and my old fears aren't necessary anymore."

"Anna—"

Whatever Evan had meant to say was lost as their waitress approached their table, and after their order was taken he turned to other topics, lighter topics that led to easy, uncomplicated dinner conversation. Anna had thought she'd never feel this freedom, this lightness, while talking to any man. But, she realized, their weeks of friendship in the hospital had laid the groundwork for the ease she now felt around Evan, an ease that even her growing awareness of him as a desirable man, a man not entirely out of reach for her now, could not totally dispel.

Evan ordered wine with their meal, a local vintage he told her he had heard of but had not been able to find during his travels, and that, too, contributed to the ease she felt with him, an ease that led their conversation to their pasts.

Anna told him about her Uncle Toby, his love for fine wood, and how much help he had been to her after the deaths of her parents—her father from a massive heart attack, and her mother from complications of pneumonia only a few months later—and with raising a young sister who was just entering adolescence when her life was torn apart.

And Evan told her about Jed Claymore's dream and of the challenges he had faced establishing his freight line, about the dangers of hauling freight on riverboats and in wagons across a wild land, and he told her about growing up in the house Jed had finally built in Fort Smith, on the road that led to the river, and eventually to the ferry across the river to Van Buren.

But Anna didn't tell Evan about always feeling she had been a disappointment to her beautiful parents, or how she had always felt they looked upon Lisa as vindication, as proof they were not as defective as their first child might indicate.

And she noticed that Evan did not once mention his mother.

"And what about Jane?" Anna asked, laughing as he related yet another childhood prank. "How did she react when you were running roughshod over Jed Claymore's mansion, sliding down the banisters and climbing up the drapes."

Evan's smile slipped slightly. "Pretty good," he said. "While she was there."

"I don't understand. I thought she had been with your family forever."

He shook his head. "No. She left when my father died. I hadn't seen her for almost twenty years when she showed up on my doorstep last month."

"Well," Anna told him, "I'm certainly glad she came back. And I know you must be, too. I can sense the affection between you."

"Affection?" Evan asked, as though the thought had never occurred to him. A frown dragged his brows together momentarily. "I don't think so. Remembered affection, maybe. And I respect her as a competent worker."

He took her hand then, clasping it lightly, and all thoughts of Jane Mudge and Eileen Claymore fled as she felt a tingling awareness of Evan, an awareness that spread from their joined hands until it gripped her entire body as completely as her tension had earlier.

"I'd better get you home," Evan told her. "It's been a long day for you."

Miraculously, Anna was able to hide her growing physical awareness of Evan from him. On the ride home, she was even able to laugh at a humorous story he told her, able to relate an equally funny misadventure of her own.

They were still laughing when they pulled into the parking area behind her shop. Jane's car was gone. The entire building was dark except for the glow of a light through her upstairs kitchen doors.

"Thank you, Evan," she said, turning toward him in the darkness of the car. "I can't remember having a better time than today." Then, afraid that if she didn't reach for the door handle she'd reach for him, Anna turned to leave the car. Evan's hand on her arm stopped her.

"I'll walk you upstairs," he told her.

Before she could argue, he was out of the car and around to her door, opening it for her.

"If you walk me upstairs, then I'll have to come back down with you to lock up. It's all right for me to go in alone, Evan. I've been doing it for years."

"You haven't had workmen crawling all over your building for all those years," he said. "They might have left tools or supplies out you could trip on. Besides, Jane's not there. Something could be wrong. You can lock up as we go in, and I'll come down the outside stairs—but I am going in with you, Anna."

No tools littered the stairs, no supplies lay scattered to sabotage her route, no bogeyman lay in wait—but Anna felt danger crackling in the air as Evan guided her through the darkened building and up the stairs, with his hand lightly at her back.

Anna had never invited a man to her apartment at night before.

And since Bill Hatfield had unwrapped her face less than a week ago, all the rules she had painstakingly acquired and adopted for herself had changed.

And she wanted more changes.

She'd admitted to herself that she loved Evan Claymore. Now she admitted to herself that she wanted him. In spite of the dangers wanting him might bring. In spite of the fact that he was so far out of her reach. In spite of everything in her past that told her she couldn't have him or love him in any way other than the one they had already established.

The apartment was not as dark as she had feared. A few lamps had been lit in various rooms, casting glowing warmth throughout the shadows. They walked directly through to the kitchen, though, where one small light had been left on above the stove, and found Jane's note propped against Anna's antique cake server, which now held a beautifully frosted, towering chocolate layer cake.

I'm sorry, but I have to attend to a personal emergency—nothing for you to worry about. I'll be back first thing in the morning.

Anna read the note and handed it to Evan. He read it silently and handed it back to her.

"Well, I guess I'd better go."

"Evan, I..."

"What is it, Anna?"

The dim light in the room reflected from Evan's eyes. The setting, the light, the circumstances, were all different, but Anna was thrown back in memory to the first time she had seen him. He was still the sexiest man she had ever laid eyes on. And he was no more aware of her as a woman than he had been that day in the hospital. She might as well still be wrapped up like the Mummy's bride.

Evan had told her she was beautiful, had told her that other men were looking at her; the woman she had seen in the mirror that morning had been beautiful. Why, then, was he looking at her as though she were just... just Anna?

And why didn't she know how to let him know she was attracted to him? Other women knew how. Neither Lisa nor, probably, Eileen, would hesitate to let someone like Evan know she was interested in more than a "Well, gee, thanks, it's been a pleasant evening."

Anna read books, she watched television, she had seen the loving interaction between Bill and Grace Hatfield, and on occasion she had even seen her sister going after a man who attracted her, but the only way she knew to let Evan know how she felt about him was simply to tell him.

And she wasn't brave enough to do that. She might never again be brave enough to let herself be that vulnerable.

Perhaps she ought to offer him some cake—Jane had apparently left it there for that reason—but she couldn't do that either, now. She knew he had no way of reading her thoughts. A moment ago she had almost hoped he could. Now, perversely, she was glad he couldn't, glad he couldn't poke around and pry into the embarrassment and sense of inadequacy she was once again too aware of feeling.

And he was standing there as though waiting for something. What? Oh, yes, she remembered. An answer. "What is it, Anna?" he'd asked, maybe so long ago that even he'd forgotten the question.

"Nothing," she said, opening the atrium doors and stepping out onto the balcony.

It wasn't late; it was just barely fully dark. The surrounding buildings, the pavement below, even the air, still held the heat of day, but a mild breeze whispered across the balcony, ruffling the leaves of the rejuvenated honeysuckle growing in wooden tubs. She heard Evan's footsteps behind her and knew she had to turn to face him. "Thank you for a wonderful day," she said, forcing a smile as she turned. "I don't know how I would have managed the car negotiations without your help." Now her smile faltered as she realized how close Evan had come, how close she stood to his wonderfully sculptured, now-unsmiling mouth, to the chest that had more than once shielded her, to arms that had held her in consolation but never in passion. *And never would.*

Now her voice faltered, too. "And I don't believe I've ever enjoyed dining out as much as I did tonight."

"Anna." He took another step closer and raised his hands to cup her face. "You have the most gloriously expressive eyes. They were the first thing I noticed about you. The day of your surgery, when I was standing by your bed, your eyes smiled at me. They haven't smiled since we left the restaurant."

"You must have an active imagination, Evan. Uncle Toby and Lisa both told me I was an almost perfect poker player, because I never gave anything away."

"Oh, Anna." His fingers crept into her hair as he continued to hold her face captive. "Didn't they ever look?"

He was looking. And Anna was afraid he was seeing far past her eyes, into her soul—seeing far more than she wanted him to, seeing secrets she knew she must keep.

"Don't . . ." she whispered.

"I won't hurt you, Anna. I swear to God, I won't hurt you. But I have to do this. I think I've had to since the moment I met you."

He angled his head and closed the scant distance that separated them, and then his lips, his wonderful mobile lips, were on hers, as they had been in countless half-remembered dreams, *drinking* from her, for that was the only way she knew to describe Evan's curious combination of need and hesitation. She felt her heart swelling as her body urged her closer to his, felt long-dormant senses and nerve endings coming painfully to life.

He pulled slightly away from her, once again looking deep into her eyes. "Kiss me," he murmured. "Kiss me as though you mean it. Give me that much."

"Evan . . ." She lifted her hands to his face, pulling him to her. For a moment she was in his arms, and he in hers, for a moment they were close enough that she felt his arousal and the heady thrill of the thought that *she* had caused this need in him. But when her mouth parted beneath his, she felt his hands tighten on her shoulders as he again pulled away from her.

"I'm sorry," he said, twisting away from her and grasping the balcony railing. "I shouldn't have done that."

"Evan . . ."

He turned back to her and trailed his fingers across her lips. "Lock yourself in," he said softly. "I'll talk to you tomorrow."

And then he was gone, so quickly that she had no time to wonder what she had done wrong until after she had locked herself safely in her once-again-spotless, once-again-lonely apartment.

"I know what you're doing."

Evan had been summoned to Eileen's condominium early that morning. She hadn't liked Great-great-grandpa's drafty old house, which was fortunate, because Evan's father had been almost feudal in his beliefs. He couldn't entail the property, so he'd done the next best thing—locked it securely in trusts for his son. But that was an old topic, and one not likely to drag Eileen from her bed at this hour.

Surprised by the early summons, Evan was only confused by his mother's words.

"And I must say, in principle, I approve," Eileen continued. "If the little nobody is in love with you, she's not going to want to cause you a great deal of damage. But must you be so obvious about your apparent interest in this woman? At least three people called me last night wanting to know the identity of the new woman in your life. And, of course, you had failed to let me know, so I had no idea who she was until I talked to Tom Fairmont."

How typical of his mother to assign ulterior motives to his friendship with Anna. And how typical of her to try to fill him with guilt for not having consulted her.

"Is that why you called me over here this morning?" he asked.

"Evan." His mother's voice firmed, losing all traces of the gentle chiding with which she had begun the conversation. "I know that you and Margo have had a disagreement."

Evan set his fragile china cup on the glass-topped coffee table and stood up. "You might as well have enjoyed your sleep this morning and not wasted my time. That is a closed subject."

"I know you and Margo have had a disagreement," Eileen repeated. "I know that she will be a most suitable wife for you, even without her family's interest in Voyager Airlines. I also know you are working diligently on the transfer of my interest in Riverland Trucking. I wouldn't want you to jeopardize either of these marvelous opportunities for a passing, totally unsuitable attraction."

"Why, Eileen," he said with a cool, quiet calm he was far from feeling, "that sounds suspiciously like a threat."

Eileen's practiced laugh was as false as Evan's calm. "Oh, darling boy, of course it isn't. I have only your best interests at heart."

When Evan left his mother's house, he left with the same sense of frustration and anger with which he left most encounters with her. But it wasn't her implied blackmail which troubled him. Trust Eileen to believe he had ulterior motives in seeing Anna. But, of course, he'd known she would. Just as he had known that any number of his so-called friends would think that. But would Anna? No. Of that he could be equally sure. Anna was too open and honest in her dealings with others even to see guile and deception when it was actually present; she wouldn't assign it to him without reason.

"I know what he's doing."

Anna had finally gotten to her clay, had pulled the wheel into position, had closed the workroom doors on workmen and Jane Mudge and disturbing thoughts and feelings about Evan Claymore, and had begun work on a series of her always popular heavy bowls when Lisa intruded.

Anna glanced up, but didn't lift her hands from the bowl taking shape on the wheel. "What who is doing, Lisa? And good-morning to you, too."

"Claymore. He let me think he was just an insurance adjuster, because he knew I'd see through him in a minute."

Anna's normally sure hands slipped, and her growing bowl became once again just a lump of clay. She sighed, knowing the only way she could return to work was first to listen to Lisa. She stopped the wheel, dumped the clay back into safe storage and walked to the nearby sink to wash her hands.

She scrubbed the clay from beneath her nails and picked up a towel as she turned and leaned against the counter. "Evan *told* you he was an insurance adjuster?"

Lisa frowned at her, almost as though she had been expecting some reaction other than amused disbelief. "Of course he didn't actually *say* he was an adjuster, but when I asked him if he was with the insurance company, he..."

"He what, Lisa?"

"He...he... Oh, for goodness sake, I'm not the one on trial here."

"I didn't know that anyone was."

"Come on, Anna, grow up. Why do you think he's spending so much time around you?"

That was a good question, one Anna had asked herself, but not one she wanted to discuss with her sister. "For someone who's made herself very scarce lately, you seem awfully aware of my activities."

"The whole town is aware of your activities. He's making a fool of you, playing up to you so you won't sue him and wind up owning all his earthly possessions."

Anna dropped the towel and clutched the edges of the cabinet. "Don't you think," she asked softly, "can you not conceive, that he's spending time with me because we enjoy each other's company?"

Lisa laughed, and her laugh told Anna just how naive, how ignorant, how manipulable, her sister thought she was. Anna closed her eyes and tried to shore up her internal armor against the pain of that laugh, but Lisa's words slashed through her weakened defenses. "Evan Claymore is a wealthy, sophisticated, well-traveled, handsome man, a man who can have his pick of women on two continents—"

"So what would he want with Anna Harrison?" Anna finished for her. She twisted around so that she faced the wall, unable any longer to look on her sister's beautiful face. "What would he want with a woman whose own family was ashamed to be seen with her?"

Suddenly all the old taunts, the old pain, the old shame, rose up in Anna's heart, boiling around with the neglect and casual abuse Lisa had shown her in the past year, and she knew that if her sister stayed, words might be said that could never be taken back, wounds might be opened that could never heal.

"I think you had better go," she said tightly.

"Anna—"

"I think you had better go. Now."

Seven

Late that afternoon, Evan finally freed himself from the trucking company and drove east, across the river to Van Buren.

Anna's small alleyway was still filled with work trucks and now a late-model, only slightly worn minivan, but he squeezed the Chevy into a parking space and stepped from the car, stretching, feeling the tension of the day easing from him. He glanced up, noticed that the balcony doors were open and hurried up the outside stairs, directly to the apartment.

Jane met him at the door and handed him a glass of iced tea. He felt a brief pang of disappointment that Anna had not been the one to meet him, to hold out a thirst-quenching drink to him after a long day, to smile at him. He dismissed that thought as unreasonable and uncharacteristic of him, and leaned back against the counter, feeling more tension ease from him as the comfort of Anna's kitchen and the undeniably welcoming aroma of something delicious cooking in a bright blue pot on her kitchen range wrapped themselves around him.

A tall, graceful vase stood on the small kitchen table, elegant, but out of place in the homey kitchen. Evan recognized the art nouveau lines, reminiscent of an Erté design or a Mucha print.

"This is beautiful," Evan said, gesturing toward the vase. "Is it Anna's work?"

"Yes. She told me she made it for her bedroom when she first moved in. It's perfect in there, but she's giving it to her across-the-street neighbor."

Evan felt a small tug of memory. "The dried-flower lady?"

"You've met Mrs. Richmond? I didn't think you ever..."

"I met her before I knew who Anna really was. She seems nice enough, just not quite the Erté type."

"She's a closet romantic, too." Jane turned to the counter and began gathering dishes and silver. "Evan," she asked abruptly, "what did that child do before we came into her life?"

By *child*, Jane had to mean Anna. But what did Jane mean by before *we* came into her life? She seemed quick to include herself in what could be no more than a temporary affiliation for her, and though Evan had tried to forget, he remembered how easily she could ignore one of those. That memory brought back other memories, flaring anger he'd thought long ago resolved and sharpening his words.

"Do?" he asked. "I imagine she did the same thing she's going to do after we leave it," he said. "*We* do have that kind of history, don't we, Jane?"

Jane turned to the stove, lifting the lid on the blue pot and slamming it forcefully back into place "I will not be forced out of anyone's life ever again. Do you hear me, Evan Claymore?"

Evan carefully placed his tea glass on the counter. "I hear you, Jane, I just don't understand what you're talking about. I think you'd better explain."

"No." Jane gave the range burner one final adjustment, and when she again turned toward Evan, her face was composed. "No. What I had better do is tell you what happened here today.

"Lisa came by this morning. I don't know what she said to Anna, because they were in Anna's workroom. She didn't stay long, but Anna quit working when Lisa left. She came upstairs, all agitated and antsy, but wouldn't tell me what happened, and then she decided that she had to go visit her neighbor, because Mrs. Richmond hadn't come over to see her and Anna was afraid she might have done something to offend her. Can you imagine that child offending anybody?

"Well, she asked me to go with her, said I probably would enjoy meeting her neighbor. Mrs. Richmond had seen Anna coming and going the past few days, so she wasn't surprised by Anna's appearance. In fact, she seemed genuinely pleased. She was also pleased that Anna had come out of that dark depression she'd suffered so long at the hospital, because all of the neighbors had really worried about her and would have come to see her if she'd just let them."

"What—"

Jane held up her hand, silencing him. "There's more. It seems that Mrs. Richmond was offended—well, disappointed is more like it—because Anna hadn't said anything to her about her caring for her plants all these months. She knew she hadn't been able to give them the care Anna would have, but she'd expected *some* word or gesture.

"When we came back over here, Anna brought that vase out of her bedroom, said Mrs. Richmond had always admired it, and then she looked at me in that way she has that just makes your heart hurt and said, 'Why?' Of course, I couldn't answer that. And then she said, 'Did she lie about everything?' But before I could even begin to understand what she meant by that, she'd gone back downstairs and closed herself up in her workroom.''

Anna hadn't been crying; Evan knew that was a luxury she rarely allowed herself. But her eyes looked haunted, wounded in a way he had seen before, in a way he never wanted to see again. He closed the door on the rest of the building and leaned back against it.

Her wax sculpture rested on the table in front of her, but even to him it was obvious she had done no more work on it. Her account books lay scattered on a nearby table. The plastic tub she used for storing working clay sat closed and abandoned beside the potter's wheel she had not yet cleaned.

And as she looked at him, her heart and so much pain in her eyes, it was all he could do to maintain his casual slouch by the door.

"Lisa said…" Her voice was soft, almost too soft to hear. As though realizing that, Anna hesitated, tossed her head back proudly and began again. "Lisa said the only reason you're spending time with me is so that I won't sue you and take all your earthly possessions."

Only that morning Evan had convinced himself Anna would not believe that of him, *could* not believe that of him. He forced his fists to unclench, forced his body to remain casually posed, forced his voice to remain calm, although he couldn't quite achieve any lightness in his words. "My mother thinks the same thing. Do you?"

"Do you think I want more from Riverland than what was taken from me?"

Evan shook his head. Most other women might have, he suspected. But not the one—proud, fragile, and strangely defiant—who faced him over a delicate wax sculpture. He didn't understand how, or even why, he knew this about her,

but he did know it. "No. I don't believe you're capable of
that kind of greed."

Her lashes dropped to hide the expression in her eyes from
him, and her shoulders lost some of their defiance. "Thank
you," she said. "And I don't think you're capable of the
kind of deception that would be necessary for you to lead
me on only to protect your money."

Her voice lacked the conviction of his. But he would take
what she gave him. He had to.

And he had to be that honest with her. "Oh, I am,
Anna." Her eyes widened; her mouth parted slightly in
shocked surprise. "But not with you. Never with you."

"And that's...that's what I don't understand." Her hand
went unconsciously to her cheek, closing over the invisible
scar that went so much deeper than mere skin.

Evan wanted to yank her hand away from her face; he
wanted the skill of a surgeon to remove the emotional
wounds her birthmark had left. He wanted to fold Anna in
his arms and surround himself with her warmth and caring
and, yes, beauty. He wanted to bury himself in the sweet-
ness of her body until it was impossible to tell where he
ended and she began. He wanted to feel her arms and those
glorious legs of hers wrapped around him, holding him close
and loved and needed. He wanted to hear her voice calling
his name, only his name, in passion and satisfaction.

Afraid she would read all he wanted in his eyes, he looked
away from hers, at the sculpture. The delicate butterfly had
only partially emerged from its cocoon. Did Anna recognize the symbolism? He could take that butterfly, rip it from
its protective shell, and either free it or damage it irrepara-
bly. Evan had always gone directly after what he wanted,
never hesitating, never pausing to consider any but the most
elemental effects of his action. Now, with Anna, he found
he had to pause.

"You don't understand how I could enjoy being with
someone as talented, as caring, as *genuine,* as you are? You

don't understand why I would rather be here, in the warmth of your home, enjoying your laughter, and your quick wit, and your hospitality, instead of in my own empty house? You don't understand why I would rather be with a person who never lies, even when it hurts her to speak the truth, rather than with people who think lies are simply another tool of business?"

"Evan, I..." Slowly her hand slid from her face. Her eyes remained troubled, but no longer seemed wounded. "Thank you," she said.

Again Evan shook his head. He didn't understand where his words had come from, or where he had found the truth behind them. He didn't understand, fully, the hold on him this woman could maintain simply by not demanding anything of him. And he was very much afraid he never would. "No," he said. "Thank *you.*"

August became September with few visible outward signs of change. The weather was still muggy, still oppressive. The major work was completed on her building, but the finishing touches still had to be made.

After the painful acceptance that most of her cash reserves had been depleted by her sister's gross incompetence, Anna had come to another, almost as painful, conclusion. Henry Johnston, her accountant, a man she had trusted since her college days, a man who, because of the responsibility Anna had had no choice but to delegate to him, must have been aware of Lisa's activities.

She'd had to scale down the amount of stock she ordered for Christmas in keeping with her new financial circumstances, but she had worked steadily at her potter's wheel, so her back shelves were beginning to resemble the well-stocked storage she had always maintained.

She missed Kate Dobbins, but Kate had jumped at the opportunity of a job in Houston that came up as a result of the medical conference she had attended. And Bill and

Grace Hatfield had jumped at the opportunity of a long-overdue vacation as soon as the last of their preschool-age children got over the chicken pox.

Anna worked at her wheel, she worked in her shop, she worked with her plants. Outwardly, at least to her, her life seemed to have changed very little.

Inwardly, she felt as though everything about her were new and different.

People actually looked at her now, made eye contact with her. A man had flirted with her at the service station the first time she filled the tank of her new minivan. And Evan enjoyed being with her. Anna Harrison of the clay-stained clothes and roughened hands.

Jane had refused to leave, staying on to help Anna in the apartment and in the shop with the opening crowd of curious customers and acquaintances, easing Anna's escape when the curiosity seemed more about her appearance than about her work.

"But I can't afford to pay you a fraction of what you're worth," Anna had told her.

"I know that," Jane said.

"But what about Evan's house? What—" Dismayed, Anna realized what she should have weeks before. "Evan is paying you, isn't he?"

Jane captured her hand and held it in both of hers. "When I work for Evan, I let him pay me. That's the only way he knows to reward someone, or to accept something from someone. That's the only way he would let me back in his life. When I am here, I'm not working for Evan, I'm here because I want to be. In essence, I'm working for me. That's the only way I will work, ever again, because I learned a long time ago how imprisoning having to depend on someone else for wages can be. I'm not wealthy by anyone's standards other than my own, but I have enough for my needs. So if you need to pay me, if this is something you have to do, compute my hours on the basis of any part-time help on Main Street. And subtract my room and board. All right?"

Anna fought back a laugh, then realized the futility of fighting it and gave it its freedom. "Evan told me when I met you that no one *let* you do anything, and that I wouldn't be able to stop you from doing what you thought was necessary. I didn't believe him. I guess I should have."

For only a second, Anna glimpsed an old, remembered sadness in Jane's eyes, before she, too, laughed, squeezed Anna's hand in hers before releasing it, and returned to her self-appointed task of dusting shelves. "And don't you forget it, either."

He ought to leave her alone, ought to get out of her life before she, with her inherent generosity, convinced herself she felt more for him than she did. Every day, Evan told himself that. Every day, he considered returning to the known stresses of his Virginia office or the new challenges of World Parcel's European headquarters and leaving Riverland and all its problems to his mother and her cast of incompetents, leaving Anna and the entire new set of problems she was causing him to the tender mercies of Jane Mudge, leaving Jane Mudge and the memories of a small boy who'd thought he'd found one person in the whole world to love him to return to the devil, to whom he'd long ago consigned her.

And every day he found himself drawn back to Van Buren, to a shop that was elegant in its simplicity, to an apartment that was filled, almost overwhelmingly so, with beauty and comfort and a sense of home that he had not known since his childhood, if even then, and to a woman who had never demanded anything from him and yet, by her very essence, demanded everything.

He parked in the porte cochere of Jed Claymore's brick mansion and let himself in through a heavy oak door, into a dark side hallway. Just inside, he stopped and sniffed, at last identifying the aromas of lemon oil and fresh flowers.

He frowned—irrationally, he knew. Mudge and her minions had been here again.

And it was his own fault. When she'd shown up on his doorstep, refusing to go away, he'd been so shocked at seeing her again, he'd acted like the boy he'd been the last time he saw her. Well, not quite. He'd been a little more imperious than that boy. He'd gestured around him, at Great-great-grandpa Jed's timeworn dream, and commanded, "Make this place livable again."

And it seemed that was what she was doing. She'd hired gardeners to renovate the neglected lawns, and painters and paperhangers he'd never seen, who miraculously completed whatever task she set them to in his absence. She'd let light into the gloomy rooms.

He went into the library, which he had commandeered for his home office. He found the flowers there, as well as a cleaned and freshened Oriental rug he remembered from the attic. His massive walnut desk gleamed from lemon oil and care. The room radiated opulence and elegance and old money. Except for one thing. He walked to the imposing bronze statue standing in the corner and lifted a decrepit hat from its noble head. His fishing cap. He hadn't thought about it in years—not since his father's death—except to wonder who had thrown it away.

Evan bowed his head, holding that cap, and remembered how he'd worn that cap, bicycling down to the river with a rod and tackle box he kept hidden in the back of the garage. Always alone—until he reached the river and the kids from a less affluent neighborhood who gathered there, not realizing who he was or what a treat it was for him to be with them.

Make this place livable again, he'd commanded. But had he realized he was asking for something he'd never really known?

The red light on his answering machine was blinking. He returned the hat to the statue's head and patted it once before settling into the leather desk chair and loosening his tie. He pushed the button to play his messages, and his mother's voice spilled into the room.

"Evan, I simply can't wait any longer. I'm having a small dinner party to try out my new face. And to renew some valuable contacts. You must be there. And try to be on good behavior. You have developed the most irritating practice of annoying our friends. Eight o'clock."

His mother's presence lingered in the room long after her voice fell silent, disturbing the warmth and welcome he had felt when he first arrived. Until his glance fell on his cap, perched irreverently on a bronze that had cost as much as some fishing lakes. He felt a grin lifting the heavy mood his mother seemed always to sink him into. "Irritating practice," he murmured reflectively. He hadn't been aware of being particularly irritating, or particularly different, in the last several weeks, but maybe he had been. Maybe the inherent honesty of one deceptively fragile woman was working its way into his psyche.

Dinner for a dozen or so at his mother's, or an alternative that came easily to mind? That was no contest. He picked up the phone and punched out a number he had easily committed to heart.

Her voice was breathless, as though she had grabbed for the phone in the midst of some task.

"Anna?"

"Evan!"

He heard the welcome in her voice, could imagine the sparkle in her eyes, the smile that would be softening her beautiful mouth.

"I have a craving for a kitchen-size pizza with most of the kitchen on it," he told her. "Would you and Jane like to share it with me?"

*   *   *

Jane stayed only long enough to pluck one slice of pizza from the box. "I've set the dining room table for you two, but I have to leave. I have tickets to the Fort Smith symphony orchestra's first concert of the season," she said between bites of pizza. "And a friend and I are going out to a late dinner afterward, so I might just spend the night at her place. I really hate to drive at night."

Since when? Evan wanted to ask, but he realized that he didn't know if Jane hated to drive at night or not, that he didn't know any number of things about this surprising woman who had returned to his life as abruptly as she had left it. He glanced at her sharply. What about all her admonitions to him about not hurting Anna? And why did it seem that she was developing a habit of leaving him alone with the very woman she seemed determined to protect from him?

But he kept all his questions to himself, and after Jane left he helped Anna carry the pizza and the bottle of local wine he had hunted up into the dining room.

A crystal bowl of salad, two place settings of china and a many-branched candelabra waited at one end of an immense cherry table. The table and matching pieces— buffet, cabinet and server—were graceful, beautiful, but somehow out of character with the life-style he knew Anna maintained.

"These were my grandmother's," Anna told him, as though sensing his unspoken questions. "Uncle Toby sent them to live with me when he moved out of his house into an apartment."

"They're lovely," Evan said, refusing to question her about her odd phrasing or about how many holiday meals she had taken alone in a dining room that could easily and appropriately contain the dinner party his mother would soon be presiding over.

Idiot! he admonished himself. Anna hadn't been completely alone. She knew half the town. She'd had her Uncle Toby until a year ago. And, as much as he disliked what he'd seen of Lisa, he had to admit Anna had also had her sister. He had no business trying to make this woman into a martyr; she hadn't been one, and she wouldn't appreciate his thinking she had. And, he admitted as he slid the box of pizza onto a waiting trivet, *he* was the one who more often than not had dined in solitary splendor.

"Thank you," Anna told him as she took two delicate wineglasses from the china cabinet. She placed them on the table, and for the first time Evan noticed that she seemed uneasy in the intimate setting Jane had so blatantly arranged.

"Would you be more comfortable in the kitchen?" Evan asked. "We don't really need to use your china and crystal for pizza."

"No. I like using beautiful things. That's why I have them. It's just..." She glanced around the dimly lit room. "I..."

"Would this help?" Evan asked, walking to the doorway and twisting the dial on the light switch until light from the ornate converted gaslight fixture overhead flooded even the corners of the room.

Anna smiled at him from across the expanse of the table, but she didn't seem any more at ease.

And why? Evan wondered. Surely she realized he knew this romantic stage set had been engineered by Jane. Unless Anna wanted the romance and didn't know how to accept it, how to ask for it. How to react once thrown into it.

Fool, he told himself. He should have left the lights low. After all Anna had given him, he could have given her at least this much. He couldn't very well dim them again, though, not without looking twice the fool he already felt. The humor of the situation struck him then, and he fought to keep from laughing at himself. Imagine him, of all peo-

ple, acting like a gauche adolescent. His mother would be
rendered speechless, and Margo would know undeniably
what she had only suspected since he had broken their engagement—that someone other than the carefully con-
structed facade occupied his body.

Oh, God, Anna thought miserably. For days she had
wanted nothing more than to be alone with Evan, quietly,
privately, in a situation where they might explore the emotions she felt building within her, where they might explore
the physical attraction she knew they both felt. But now that
they had been plunged into just such a setting, she'd pan-
icked. And Evan knew it. And he...oh, Lord, he was
laughing.

"Here," she said, picking up the bottle of wine and
thrusting it across the table. "You'll have to open this. I always butcher the cork."

He took the bottle from her, his dark brows drawing together in question, and his laughter faded. "I was just
wondering what people I know would think if they saw me
in this situation."

She felt herself shriveling inside, but she had to ask. She
stood calmly, and with all the pride and dignity she could
muster. "And just what is this situation?"

He looked at her intently. Though they were still separated by the width of the table, she knew that he again saw
too deeply, but she couldn't turn away.

"Oh, Anna," he said softly, looking from her to the bottle, then back to her face. "Don't you know? For one of the
few times in my life, I'm unsure. I don't know what to say.
I don't know how to act. And those other few times? Lady,
those other few times have been when I was with you, too."

Anna felt her heart lighten; she felt the smile that softened her face and her eyes. But this kind of intimacy was too
new, and too treasured, for her to know how to react. In-

stead, she drew on old patterns—the seemingly light humor that had sustained her so well.

"Perhaps I should get us a deck of cards," she said softly, her smile and the gently teasing lilt of her voice taking all sting and all sarcasm from her words. "You never seemed to be unsure of yourself while you were cheating me at gin rummy."

Evan's answering smile was equally gentle, equally teasing. "Perhaps you're right."

Anna looked around the spacious room and shrugged, but picked up plates and glasses and forks and napkins, and stacked them on the pizza box before picking it up. "And perhaps you'd enjoy this more in the living room, watching whatever it is they're featuring on the sports network tonight."

Nothing on the sports network tempted them, but they settled on Anna's chintz sofa and happily fell into a rerun of a National Geographic special on PBS. Anna had read about the places featured; Evan had visited several of them. They shared bits and pieces of knowledge that the special didn't cover, that one of them didn't know, until the program was over, the pizza was consumed, and the wine was low in the bottle.

Evan stretched contentedly, wondering when he had shed his shoes, and when his feet had found their way onto Anna's coffee table. He knew when she had settled next to him, her head leaning back over his outstretched arm, her slight weight a warm treasure against his side; he'd been aware of her, pleasantly and yet almost painfully, since the moment she did so.

But was she aware of it? There was no artifice, no guile, no coy pretending, with Anna. If she seemed at ease beside him, she was at ease—not preparing a seduction or planning a merger or even practicing a little one-upmanship.

And could she be aware of where she was, of what she was doing to him, if she were at ease? It didn't seem likely.

He rolled his head to the right to look at her. Aware of his movement, she turned her head to face him. He knew the moment she became aware of how close she had come to him. He saw it in her eyes, saw the almost immediate, instinctive withdrawal, saw her fight that and, finally, saw her awakening desire.

And he knew the moment she became aware that he was going to kiss her, because it was the same moment he became aware that there was no way in hell he could not do just that.

Eight

Anna's glorious eyes, the same eyes that had smiled at him, had welcomed him, had laughed with him, now darkened in awareness and desire as Evan lifted his hand to her cheek. Her lips softened and parted and whispered a soft sigh as they met his.

He'd wanted to be gentle with her, to give her pleasure, to show her that he, too, could give without demanding anything in return. But the moment she turned in his arms, surrendering against him, the need in him threatened to overpower him, as it had threatened the last time he held her close, as it had actually done in his troubled dreams.

He had never wanted a woman as much as he wanted Anna Harrison. And no woman had ever felt so right in his arms as she did. Evan wanted this to be right for Anna, too, but her slender body was so responsive, her skin was so silky and tempting, her small breasts were so perfect in his hands, beneath his mouth, and her hands, her strong, supple hands, trailed liquid fire and exquisite pleasure wherever she allowed them to wander.

Anna had only dreamed of, never truly believed in, the maelstrom of emotions buffeting her, from within and without, as she surrendered herself to the mastery she sensed in Evan's embrace. When he groaned her name against her mouth and pulled her still closer to him, she again felt his need, as she had before, but this time his touch held no hesitation. And after that first brief, shocked moment when she had realized he would at last kiss her, neither had hers.

He held her, as she had dreamed of him holding her. He touched her, as she had dreamed of him touching her. He kissed her, as she had never dared to dream of him kissing her. And she was free to hold him, to touch him, to kiss him. For this night, no matter where it led, she was free to show Evan Claymore how much she loved him.

And she did love him. She'd thought sometimes, alone at night, that her heart would burst with the need to express that love. Now she poured it out to him with her hands, her lips, her breath.

His breathing was harsh in the quiet of the room, and his weight was a blessed burden. She knew somehow he would not welcome a declaration of her love, but she was incapable of saying anything other than his name, which she did, repeating it over and over, praising and pleading.

Her blouse lay open, spread around her on the floral chintz sofa; her body glowed—with the sheen of perspiration the shared heat of their bodies had generated, and from the moisture left by Evan's gentle, erotic laving. His fingers trailed across her ribs, igniting and inciting small explosions and riots throughout her.

"Evan..." she murmured.

And suddenly he twisted away from her.

"Evan?"

She heard him expel a harsh breath as he turned to sit on the edge of the sofa, elbows on his knees, head in his hands.

"Evan?" she asked again, rising on the couch, reaching to touch him, and even she could hear the pain and confusion in her voice.

He turned to her then, reached out with trembling fingers to gather her blouse about her, and drew her into his arms. He held her close against him, and she heard the thundering of his heartbeat as he rested his chin on her head and just sat there, saying nothing, doing nothing but holding her and breathing in deep, painful breaths.

"I let that get out of hand," he said finally, still holding her.

Don't say you're sorry. Please, God she begged silently, *don't let him say he's sorry.*

"You don't want to make love with me?" she asked instead, proud of how calm she sounded with her face muffled against his chest.

She felt his arms tighten around her. Then he released her and began stuffing his feet back into his shoes.

"Are you protected against pregnancy, Anna? Were you going to ask me if I'm healthy? Were you going to demand that I take measures to protect you, not only against pregnancy, but against much worse? If I'd admitted I had nothing with me, do you have your own little pharmacy tucked away somewhere in this maze of an apartment?"

"No," she said, rubbing her hands against suddenly chilled arms. "No to all of it." She sat there, huddled into herself, watching his quick, jerky motions as he readied himself to leave. He looked so *angry.*

"Evan," she asked, "what's really wrong?"

"You..."

Oh, Lord, she thought, *had she said it?* Had she actually spoken the words that she felt so deeply? No, she realized almost as quickly. She had not been capable of coherent speech. But if she had, would they have affected Evan this way? Would they have chased him away?

"I what?" she asked, still quiet, still calm.

"You aren't ready for this," he said.

Her breasts still felt swollen and heavy from his ministrations; her body still ached with awakened and unfulfilled longings. She felt a wry smile lift the corner of her lips. "That's strange," she said softly. "Most of me thinks that I am."

"Anna..." He reached out as though to touch her, but dropped his arms to his side. "I'm going out through the kitchen doors. Come and lock yourself in."

Anna stood on the balcony until Evan's car disappeared around a corner, then turned back into the apartment and locked herself in. She was good at that, she thought, allowing only a moment of bitterness before directing her energy to tidying the apartment after their impromptu picnic.

Unfortunately, that took only a few minutes, not nearly long enough to dispel the frustration and unexpected grief that had descended on her with Evan's departure.

A shower didn't help, either, although she stood in it until the water from her more than adequate heater ran tepid. She grabbed up a bath sheet, this one a deep golden brown, as she stepped from the shower enclosure and found herself drawn to the antique pier glass across the room. Anna had kept few mirrors visible in her home or in her shop, but Jane had found this one stored in a back room with more of Anna's grandmother's things and had cleaned and polished it and installed it in here.

Now Anna stood before the full-length reflection of herself. What did Evan see when he looked at her? she wondered. She dropped the towel and examined herself critically. Not her face—over the years she had developed the ability to brush her teeth, comb her hair and scrub without ever seeing her face—but her body.

Anna's body was slender, almost too thin, but it had performed well for her in the past, doing what she demanded of it, and soon would do so again.

Her breasts were small, but well shaped. She'd wondered once—it seemed a lifetime ago now—if they would be sufficient to nurse a child. Young, naive, she'd even asked the university doctor, who'd only laughed and promised they would be. As he had also promised that her slender hips were not too slender for childbearing. But those were old wounds, and not under consideration here.

What had Evan seen when he looked at her? And then she saw them: crosshatchings of pale white lines. She had grown up looking at so much worse, when she forced herself to look, that she no longer saw the scars remaining from the accident after Bill Hatfield had worked his magic. But they covered areas on her legs, and on her back. Evan couldn't have seen them, they were so faint, but—Anna lifted her fingertips to the area beneath and around from her left breast—he could have felt them.

"Oh, *blast!*" she muttered.

Had Evan been disgusted by them, put off by them?

Anna sighed. She didn't think so. After all, this was the man who had continued visiting her, even knowing she looked like something from a grade B horror movie. So if he hadn't been put off by them, and she hadn't chased him off by blurting out that she loved him, what had happened?

And suddenly that, too, was as clear as the scars on her body. He'd been reminded. Reminded of the truck, of the trucking company, of his mother, probably of the fiancée he never talked about, of the insurance claim. And of the responsibility he felt toward her.

"Oh, blast," she said again, not daring to say anything stronger. "Blast, blast, *blast!*"

Anna surrendered herself to the rhythm of the potter's wheel. The lump of clay beneath her sure hands began rising, stretching, taking on a life of its own—guided by her, shaped by her, but ultimately to be something completely separate from her and barely reminiscent of its humble beginnings.

Work was no magic antidote against the loneliness of the days since Evan had walked out of her apartment and apparently out of her life, but it had helped. As, in some strange way, fending off the casual flirtation of a young man at the grocery store and later when he came to the shop, professing undying interest in the process of creating pottery, had helped. As working with her butterfly, at last reaching the stage where she could begin carefully encasing the wax in its plaster cast, had helped.

Completing the inventory for the insurance claim had filled her time, but it hadn't helped—not one bit. She'd been scrupulously honest in her claim; there was no way she could blame Riverland for more than what their truck had actually destroyed. They were not responsible for what Lisa had allowed to happen later. But filling out the endless papers had reminded her of her sister's betrayal.

And had reminded her of the crushing sense of responsibility Evan must have felt toward her.

Because she had decided that was why he had left her. And that was why he had spent so much time with her after learning who she was. After all, if the only remaining member of a woman's family couldn't bear to be around her...

Anna jerked her attention back to the fragile vase she was creating, but it was too late. The long, slender throat of the vase collapsed beneath her hands. Sighing, she stopped the wheel.

"Anna?"

With welcome relief, she heard Jane calling her. With any luck, there would be a minor problem to solve in the shop, and by the time she had done that she'd be able to get back to her wheel, or to glazing the already thrown pots, or to firing one of the kilns without the danger of ruining her work because she couldn't keep her mind on it.

"In the workroom," she called out.

Jane was smiling when she entered the workroom. "That shipment you've been expecting from Kansas is here."

Anna felt the first jolt of genuine pleasure she had known in days. "Kayce's stuff is here? Oh, Jane, you are going to love his work. Give me a minute to get this stashed away," she said as she lifted the clay from the wheel, "and I'll be right out."

Evan saw Jane talking to an intense young man as he paused just inside the rear door of the showroom. She smiled at the young man, then gave him a mock frown and, with hand gestures and soft words, shooed him out the front door. When she turned and saw Evan, her frown went from mock to real.

"It's about time you showed up around here. Where have you been for the last ten days?"

"Virginia," he said, coming on into the showroom. "Who was that young puppy?"

"That *puppy,* according to Mrs. Richmond across the street, is an old boyfriend of Lisa's. He's been hanging around Anna since the day after you left. And why didn't you bother to tell anybody you were out of state?"

"I needed some time, Jane. Not that it's any of your business. But so did Anna."

"She completed her claim."

"I know. I just left Tom Fairmont's office. She didn't ask for enough."

She looked at him sharply, and then all the belligerence went out of her. She was just a woman in late middle age, still tidy, still trim, never beautiful, but with a mature confidence that lent her a distinction beauty seldom bestowed.

But now she seemed weary, as he had never seen her weary before.

"Who do you want to punish?" she asked him. "The insurance company, or yourself?"

"I don't know what you're talking about."

"Yes, Evan, you do. But you won't admit it. No matter how much money Anna asked for, Eileen would never be touched—not in any way that matters."

Evan felt the anger, bright, hot, instantaneous. How dare this woman talk about not being *touched*. "Damn it, Jane," he all but shouted at her. "You have no right—"

"I have every right," she said, with just as much heat. "I paid for that right in ways you will never know." She whirled away from him, clutching at a shelf, but when she spoke, all heat and life had gone from her voice. "Anna's upstairs. She went up to look for something, but she's been gone so long, someone ought to check on her."

Evan found Anna at the back of her apartment, in a room filled to overflowing with boxes, outdated furniture and framed pictures. Though clean in its clutter, it was a high-ceilinged, bare-walled, drab room that showed him how hard she had worked to make her living quarters the warm, inviting home they were.

She neither saw him nor heard him as he paused outside the open door. She was sitting cross-legged on the floor beside a large trunk, staring unseeing at one of what appeared to be a number of photo albums spread out around her.

She was wearing her work clothes—clay-stained jeans and T-shirt—there was no makeup on her perfect face, and her hair had finally lost that too carefully styled salon look. She wore sandals on her long, slender feet, and although she sat with them tucked under her, he saw the gleam of bright red polish on her toenails. He smiled. Anna was beginning to experiment.

Evan's smile turned bittersweet. This was the woman he had just spent ten days in hell staying away from so that she *could* experiment. She had the right to do that, to flirt, to conquer, to try her wings like the fragile butterfly in her sculpture, to feel the heady success of being a beautiful woman. Jane had been right. He had the ability to take advantage of Anna, and the truth of Jane's words had been made startlingly, painfully clear that night in Anna's living room. Anna, this beautiful, talented, wonderfully generous woman, thought she was falling in love with him. He'd seen it in her eyes, felt it in her touch, heard it in her voice as she called out his name.

Impossible. After all she had been through, after all she had suffered at the hands of those who ought to love her, Anna still believed in something as nebulous as love.

And he wouldn't be the one to tell her it didn't exist.

So, no matter how much he wanted to lock her away so that he would be the only recipient of her loving generosity, no matter how much he wanted to be the only one for whom that glorious smile lit her eyes, no matter how much he wanted to be the one to finish awakening the dormant sensuality in her, he wouldn't be the one to do that, either.

Damn! Why had he come back?

He saw the glint of moisture in Anna's eyes then, and knew why he had come back. He couldn't stay away.

And whatever was causing her distress now, he knew he had to share it.

"Hi," he said softly from the doorway.

She looked up at him, and her eyes, her face, her whole being, seemed to glow. "Evan. You came back." She started to scramble to her feet, but he shook his head and walked toward her.

"Stay there," he said, "it looks like you're lost in family history." Reaching her side, he dropped down beside her. "Don't let me take you away from that."

"Somebody needs to," she told him. "I'm supposed to be looking for a piece of velvet for a display."

He glanced at the book and saw the open pages full of photographs of a laughing, happy, beautiful little girl. *You?* he almost asked before he realized the obvious: This child had no birthmark.

"Lisa?" he asked.

"Yes." Anna's voice softened as she reached out and caressed the pictures with gentle hands. "She was such a beautiful baby. I thought of her as mine, you know. Mine to love. Mine to care for."

He saw a stunningly attractive couple holding the child in one picture. "Your parents?"

Anna nodded and pointed to another photo, of an equally attractive man. "And this is Uncle Toby."

"They look . . . I don't know . . . familiar?"

Anna chuckled. "Harrison Wholesale Grocery?" she said. "Probably one of Riverland's original customers."

"That Harrison?"

Anna nodded. "Yep. Of course, the business passed out of the family's control when my parents died. Uncle Toby had gotten out years before—he preferred wood to canned goods. But he'd sold most of his interest in Oakcraft Furniture by then, too."

Evan turned the pages of the album while he tried to fit this new picture of Anna's background with the woman he knew. Harrison Wholesale was almost as much a tradition in the Arkansas River valley as Riverland Trucking. And Oakcraft Furniture, though a relative newcomer, had enjoyed more than moderate success. Anna should have had the money for surgery the moment the treatment became available. And Lisa should have had absolutely no reason to steal from her sister. It didn't fit.

And something else didn't make sense. He began paying more careful attention to the pages of the album. "Where are you?" he asked finally.

Anna took the book from him and closed it. "I told you before, I only have one picture of myself. I never wanted to have any taken."

Yeah, right, Evan thought. *Not even when you were too young to have any voice in the decision?*

"Come on," he said abruptly, jumping to his feet and reaching for her hand.

"Where?"

"To right a wrong, to change a pattern that should never have been, to open a new door, to indulge me."

On her feet now, she shook her head and gave him a wry grin. "Would you care to be a little more specific?"

"Oh." He supposed he hadn't actually told her. "To have your picture taken."

"Evan..." Her hand started toward her cheek. Abruptly she caught it to her mouth instead. "You can't be serious."

"Never more so. And I know just the photographer to take you to."

"I can't go to a portrait studio!" she all but wailed. "Not on the spur of the moment! I'd have to get my hair styled, do my makeup, find something to wear...."

She looked absolutely gorgeous to him, her face fresh and free of makeup, her ridiculously short hair tousled, bright red toenails peeking from the brown leather straps of her sandals, and a baggy T-shirt and faded jeans that only hinted at the lithe curves of her body. He wanted to capture her that way for all time, but he doubted she would agree with his opinion, or allow him to do so.

Shaking his head, he captured her hand. "Oh, Anna, you have to know I wouldn't take you to a place like that. But I saw a studio down the street—"

"Wendy Fuller's?"

"Maybe. Two blocks down the hill?" A place with old-fashioned sepia-toned photo portraits in one window and period furniture and costumes in the other. He'd seen numerous studios like it across the country, in almost every town tourists frequented, and it seemed to him the perfect, nonthreatening way to introduce Anna to a camera that was bound to love her.

Anna nodded, at last letting a reluctant smile play across her face.

"You know her?" Evan asked.

"Of course. All of the merchants on Main Street know each other."

"Is she any good?" he asked.

Now she laughed, a secretive, amused chuckle. "Better than you'd ever suspect."

A small bell over the door announced their entrance to the studio, and within seconds Wendy Fuller emerged from the back room, walking slowly and with the help of an ornate antique walking stick.

"You're out of the chair," Anna said with genuine pleasure.

"Told you I would be." Although giving up smoking was one of the many concessions Wendy had made to multiple sclerosis, Anna still heard the gravelly tobacco growl in the woman's voice. Wendy gave Evan a long, appraising glance and then walked around Anna, bright black eyes studying her intently. Although she looked long and hard at Anna's face, she said nothing about the birthmark or its absence.

"You don't look depressed to me."

Anna felt a flush at least as bright as the polish on her toenails rising from those nails to cover her entire body.

"I suspected *that* old dog wouldn't hunt," Wendy said, and Anna knew her photographer's eye had not missed her reaction. "But what the heck—I know depression. Even though your sister's a twit, I figured I'd give her the benefit of my doubt—maybe she knew what she was talking about, maybe you really did need to be alone.

"I guess we all figured wrong. So. How much has she hit you up for since you've been home?"

"Wendy—"

"Anna needs some portraits made," Evan said easily, rescuing Anna from hasty, unrecallable words.

Wendy glanced at him curiously, waiting.

"At least a half dozen, I think," he said. "Different poses, different periods."

"Of Anna?" she asked, and when Evan nodded, once again Wendy walked around Anna, studying her. "Oh, boy," she said, her bright eyes flashing, making Anna wonder just what she was plotting. "I have wanted to get you in my viewfinder for years. I guess you know I'd kill to have cheekbones like yours."

Anna stood perfectly still, stunned into silence. Wendy had wanted to photograph *her?* Wendy envied *her* cheekbones. Evan had just blithely ordered at least a half-dozen photographs of her, Anna Harrison? And she, who had only submitted with embarrassed ill will to posing for her driver's-license photo, had agreed? Was even looking forward to this session? And then panic freed her. "Evan, I don't—"

"Come on into the back room," Wendy said, interrupting Anna's stammering attempt to escape.

"Costumes?" Evan asked, gesturing vaguely toward the rack of period clothes.

Wendy shook her head. "Those are for the souvenir hunters, more than good enough for what they want. But for *this* session, we're going to get into my private stock. Do I get to do your makeup, too?"

"Yes," Evan told her, before Anna could speak.

"Hot damn! Then what are we waiting for? Come on."

Over the next hour, Anna was reminded—a lot—of the hours she had spent in the exclusive beauty salon. But she was also reminded of the hours she had spent sitting on the sidelines while Lisa was posed and photographed. And then she was reminded of nothing, because nothing in her life had prepared her for the laughter, for the sheer *fun,* of being costumed and pampered and posed. More than a half-dozen poses were shot; she lost track of them all. She remembered being costumed as Belle Starr, the notorious outlaw of frontier days, and as Pearl Starr, Belle's daughter, who had been almost as notorious as her mother but as a madam, not as an outlaw. Wendy had insisted on posing her as Nefertiti, the Egyptian queen, with an elaborate headdress and darkly kohled eyes. She had been a French queen, Alice in Wonderland, and a saloon dancer.

When she released Anna from the dancer's pose, Wendy walked back to her closet and took out a gray wool Confederate cavalry officer's costume and handed it to Evan.

"Hey, wait a minute," he said, laughing. "This session is for Anna, not me."

"You are the best-looking example of male flesh that has walked into my parlor in years, Mr. Claymore," Wendy said in a mock drawl. "And you are not getting out of here until I capture you on film. Now, surely there is a Rebel soldier somewhere in your family?"

Anna grinned. So she wasn't alone in her opinion of Evan's decidedly masculine attributes. "Great-great-grandpa Jed?" she asked, mimicking Wendy's horrible, honey-dripping attempt at Deep South dialogue.

Evan chuckled, but took the costume. "Either Jed or his father—the family history's not too clear on that point. But if it wasn't actually Jed, it could have been."

"And the lady in his life?" Wendy asked.

Evan's expression softened reflectively. "A dark-haired, dark-eyed Cherokee maiden from Siloam Springs," he told her.

Once again Wendy dug in her closet. "Aha!" she said triumphantly, emerging with a frontierswoman's calico dress and a dark, braided wig. "One Cherokee maiden."

But of course, while taking that photo, Wendy had to ask about Great-great-grandpa Jed.

"He founded Riverland Freight," Evan told her, while holding Anna in an exaggerated pose that threatened to break her back and made her aware of every virile inch of him.

"And built the Claymore mansion on Free Ferry Road in Fort Smith?" Wendy asked. Not waiting for an answer, she shot the photo. "Well, we'll just have to capture that aspect of him, too."

For that one, neither consulted Anna, which was all right with her; she was still recovering from being held so close in Evan's arms, though he seemed unaware of his effect on her. He and Wendy dug out a costume that seemed more that of a riverboat gambler than a freighter.

"And his lady?" Wendy asked.

Caught in the game, Evan didn't even hesitate. "A prim and proper Victorian. Her portrait is on the second-floor landing."

"Not the Cherokee maiden?" Anna asked, suddenly saddened. "What happened to her?"

Evan turned to her and touched her cheek gently. "No one seems to know. Maybe the Reb wasn't Jed after all."

They hurried into their costumes, Anna barely aware of the fine fabric of the antique gown. But she was aware that Wendy seemed quite suddenly to be tiring.

"You have to leer at me." Evan whispered from the corner of his mouth.

"What?"

"You have to leer at me. Family history *is* clear on this point. Great-great-grandma had a serious case of the hots for Great-great-grandpa."

And if Great-great-grandpa Jed had been anything like Evan, Anna had no trouble understanding why. Well, yes, maybe "trouble" was a perfect description of what her feelings for Evan could bring her.

They finished the session with laughter, but Wendy admitted she was approaching exhaustion. When Evan and

Anna had changed back into their clothes, they found her sitting behind her desk in a small office.

"We'll need two of everything," Evan told her. "Eight-by-tens, and a set of small ones. And one of those antique-looking albums for Anna, and—" he lifted an ornate silver frame from the sideboard "—something like this, if you can get it, for one of the portraits of her."

Wendy nodded happily, making notes. "I'll need about a week." She stopped speaking as Evan picked up one of several different photography books from the sideboard. They all bore the name W. J. McCauley, but Anna knew what he would find when he opened the back of the book: a small photo of a younger Wendy.

"B.M.S.," Wendy told him.

"I know your work," Evan said with quiet awe. "I wondered what had happened to you."

"Multiple sclerosis."

"I'm sorry."

Wendy measured his words. Anna knew she heard no undue pity in them. Apparently realizing that, Wendy grinned. "I was, too. But I had family here to come back to, and if I hadn't..." She gestured toward a framed photo on her desk of her and a dark, almost sinister-looking man with his arm draped protectively around her. "If I hadn't come back, I wouldn't have found Tom. And *that* would have been the tragedy of my life."

They left the studio, once again laughing, but as they started up the hill Anna was reflecting that after all Wendy had gone through, she had found someone to love, someone to love her. There was hope for her after all. Dear Lord, there was hope.

Evan draped his arm over Anna's shoulder as they walked back up the hill toward her shop. He knew he shouldn't. Now more than ever, he knew, he should let her go. Tom Fuller looked as if he had seen more hell than Evan could even imagine, but he had found Wendy, another rare treasure in what he had always thought of as a wasteland of women. The difference was, Wendy had seen enough of the world to know Tom was what she wanted.

Anna didn't have that experience. Would never have that experience as long as he hung around, taking from her. Would never have that experience until he eased himself from her life and gave her the freedom she needed. Only he wasn't sure now that he knew how to do that—or that he could, even if he did know how.

Nine

Anna sat at the small table on her rear balcony. In a concession to the brisk early-morning air, she had actually donned shoes before breakfast, and now had her canvas-clad feet propped on the iron rail of the balcony as she nursed a mug of cooling coffee.

Even protected by the sheltering buildings, the roof of her small balcony and the heavily vined honeysuckle, she felt the nip in the air that foretold the changing of the seasons. Once Anna had loved early October, with its cool nights and warm days. Once she had loved the anticipation of watching the riotous color of the changing leaves late that month, and the gradual descent of the temperature until one day, without even being aware of how it had happened, she found herself in the middle of winter.

She supposed that she would love winter when it actually arrived—she always did. That she would get caught up in the excitement of Christmas. That she would order in firewood and unpack her wool sweaters for long, cozy nights in front of the decorative wood stove in her apartment.

But now Anna realized that she had always done all those things alone.

Winter was coming, and she didn't want to be alone for this one. Not again. Not ever again.

But it looked as though she would be.

Evan never had told her the purpose for his visit the day he'd insisted on taking her to be photographed. He'd simply left her at the shop after walking her back there.

He'd been by twice since—once only a couple of days after that outing, not staying long, not saying much, and then a few days later to deliver the finished portraits.

He hadn't stayed to look at them with her.

"You're a beautiful woman," he'd told her. "If nothing else will convince you, these portraits ought to."

And then he'd left.

He had some really bad hang-up about beautiful women. Anna had known that since the beginning. But, damn it, if his truck hadn't run over her, she wouldn't *be* beautiful.

She heard Jane enter the kitchen behind her and begin preparations for the morning, and choked back a bitter laugh, not wanting to disturb the caring and surprisingly maternal woman Evan had brought into her life. But she knew, and she couldn't help acknowledging that she knew, that if Evan's truck hadn't torn up her life, he would never have noticed her; he would have paid no more attention to her than Lisa's old boyfriend Wesley—who was fast becoming a huge pest.

And maybe she was reading more into Evan's motivation than was there because she didn't want to look at the real reason he stayed away. The portraits. The damning, revealing portraits.

Wendy had done her job too well, had even captured a couple of shots Anna hadn't been aware of. One of those, the Victorian miss—without Great-great-grandpa—graced the silver frame. She had tucked the others safely away in the album. They were much too incriminating.

You have to leer at me, Evan had told her, and while Great-great-grandma wasn't exactly leering at Great-great-grandpa any more than the Cherokee maiden was leering at the Rebel officer, she, Anna, was looking at Evan with her heart in her eyes. She could see it. Wendy had to have seen it. And Evan? Well, Evan wasn't blind. And he also wasn't coming around much anymore. Damn!

"What are you doing out here this early?" Jane asked, stepping out onto the balcony with a mug of coffee in her hand.

"Swearing," Anna told her.

Jane stepped over to the railing and took a deep breath of the early-morning air. "Yes. Some mornings are good for that."

It occurred to Anna later that some mornings weren't good for anything else.

A shipment she had been promised for that day didn't come in on the daily delivery. The power company had to cut service in order to do a major repair, and plunged her entire building into darkness just as she was getting ready to fire her kiln. The trust officer from the bank, her co-trustee of Lisa's funds, telephoned to tell her that Lisa was demanding an advance on her quarterly earnings. And the elegant vase that she had worked so long and so hard on the night before—Anna herself knocked it off the workbench, shattering it.

"Go," Jane told her. "Somewhere. Anywhere. But get out of here before you destroy all your stock and drive both of us crazy."

Anna had no idea where she would go when she got into her new green minivan. Briefly she considered going into Fort Smith and looking with new eyes at the home Jed Claymore had built so many years before.

Instead, determined that she would not think about Evan again that morning, when she reached the interstate highway she turned the sporty little van east. Several miles later, she left the highway, turning south through gently rolling hills covered with well-tended grapevines. Only later, as she left one of the local wineries, did she realize that she had just purchased a generous supply of the local wine Evan was so fond of.

"So much for not thinking about him," she muttered. "Even when I'm on automatic pilot, he intrudes."

She glanced at the clock on the dashboard, gasped, and headed for home. She'd been gone well over an hour, and was at least forty-five minutes away. *And it wouldn't do anybody any good if she got herself killed trying to get back five minutes sooner.*

Smiling, Anna rolled down the driver's side window and slid a classical tape into the stereo. She wouldn't dawdle, but she would enjoy the October morning. And she *would* enjoy the rest of the day.

Her good mood lasted less than a minute after she returned home. Jane was helping an older man with a decision when Anna entered the showroom. On impulse, Anna hugged her, not caring that the man was looking on indulgently. "That was a marvelous idea," she told Jane. "Thank you."

A smile of genuine pleasure softened Jane's face as she returned Anna's brief hug, but it faded almost instantly. "I'm happy you enjoyed yourself," Jane said. "You need to get out more often."

Anna heard things unsaid in Jane's words, and saw them in her expression. "Did something else happen while I was gone?" she asked.

Jane glanced up the walnut staircase, toward the garden balcony, all traces of her smile gone. "Your sister's upstairs."

"Did she—" Remembering the customer, Anna broke off her question. Besides, from Jane's expression, she really didn't have to ask if Lisa had said something to offend Jane. "Thank you," she said instead. "I'll see what she wants."

"A thousand dollars?"

"Well, yes," Lisa said. "Of course, I really could use more, but that will get me by."

"Until when?" Anna asked.

"Until . . . well, just until."

Anna studied her sister silently. As usual, Lisa wore her clothes and jewelry as if they had been designed for her. Anna recognized the silk dress as new. And the gold-and-diamond watch. And the sapphire dinner ring. At least new in the past several months.

"For what?"

"What do you mean, for what?" Lisa asked.

"I mean, for what purpose do you need a thousand dollars?"

"For my rent and my car payment, of course. Why else would I need money?"

Right. Why else?

"I don't know how many times we've been over this, Lisa. You cannot touch the body of the trust. And you cannot have the income until the income is due. Which won't happen until the end of this month."

"Then you'll have to let me have it."

Anna reached behind her for the back of a kitchen chair. She clutched it for support, and to keep from beating on the counter in frustration. "Do you actually think I have a thousand dollars floating around that I can just hand over to you?"

"You've always been able to come up with the money when I need it."

"Lisa, listen to yourself. And think what has happened in the past year. I haven't been able to work. I don't have that kind of money."

"Right." Lisa slammed the delicate cup down on the countertop. "You always have been tighter than Scrooge with a dime. Holding the purse strings—mine, as well as yours—as though it was all yours. Well, I happen to know that you *do* have money. And I know that as soon as you finally get around to hiring a lawyer, you're going to have a lot more money. And I don't think it's too much to ask, considering that I donated months out of my life to staying in this dump, that you help me with my rent and car payment."

Anna closed her eyes and clenched her hands on the chair back before again looking at her sister. "When did you get the diamond watch?"

Lisa extended her arm and looked at the watch, smiling contentedly until she abruptly shed the smile and assumed once again the pose of pitiful supplicant. "When I ... when we ... When I saw Evan Claymore sucking up to you and realized how scared he was, how good our case really was against Riverland. I mean, I'd wanted it for ages, and suddenly there didn't seem any reason for me not to have it."

Anna felt the blow of Lisa's words, but she ignored the first of them and concentrated on what, for Lisa, had to be the heart of the matter. *"Our case?"*

"Well, yes," Lisa admitted reluctantly. "You were the one who was actually physically hurt. But we are family, and I did have to give up all my plans because you couldn't tend your shop, so I naturally assumed you'd want me to—"

Anna had a quick vision of the kind of care Lisa had given her shop and home, and she suppressed a shudder.

"I'm not hiring a lawyer," she said, interrupting her sister's attempt to justify her greed. "I've already filed my claim for actual losses." *And not counting the losses of missing stock, damaged business goodwill, and just plain taken money.* She wanted to say it, wanted to yell accusations at her sister, but she bit back those words, holding them tightly inside her, afraid they would escape.

"You *what?* Don't you know you could practically own that trucking company?"

"I don't want to own the trucking company, Lisa. I want to own my shop. And I want to own my self-respect."

"And, of course, you got a new face out of it, so I guess you're probably grateful to him for that."

Anna felt the pressure of unshed tears behind her eyes and in her throat. "I have to get back to work," she said.

"Anna!"

Lisa's incredulous cry stopped her in her careful attempt at a dignified exit from a scene that had no dignity. She turned, one brow lifted in question.

"I *need* the money. You've always given me what I need."

Anna felt a sigh building within her, felt a sorrow so deep she didn't know if she would survive it. She had always given in to Lisa—had even before her sister was born. She looked at the imperious, selfish woman across the room from her and tried to remember the beautiful, laughing baby she had been. Anna had been so excited about having a baby sister. Even at six years old, she had realized a baby wouldn't know she was ugly, wouldn't know she was deformed, wouldn't turn away from her in disgust. That a baby would love her. And the baby had. But the baby had become a child, a girl, a young woman.

Anna had lived a long time on the memory of a baby's love. She had even convinced herself it still existed. Now she wasn't sure. But Lisa was right. Anna had always given her what she needed. She couldn't stop now.

"How much is your car payment?" she asked.

Lisa named a figure that Anna recognized was at least twice as much as the actual amount. She halved it, retrieved her checkbook from her bedroom and made out of a check for that amount. "I expect this back by the first of the month. You'll have to ask your landlord to wait. If you explain your trust fund to him, he probably will. If not..." Anna hesitated. The last thing she wanted right now was to invite Lisa back into her home, but that was selfish of her. If she had room to store all of her grandmother's odd and ends, which Uncle Toby had sworn Lisa's children would someday want, she had more than enough room for Lisa herself. "If he won't wait, then you can come back here."

Lisa took the check, glanced at it without speaking and left.

Anna walked out onto the balcony and collapsed into a chair. She twisted her head and rubbed her neck, trying to ease the tension there, and lifted her face to the slight breeze. "Yes," she said, her voice soft and thickened by unshed tears. "Some afternoons are made for swearing, too."

Though dressed for dinner, Evan couldn't yet force himself to leave. He sat in his father's leather chair in the library, with the photo album open across his lap. Wendy Fuller had included the album with his pictures, even though he hadn't ordered it. She'd given him a lot more than he'd ordered. With the insight that had made her such a superb photojournalist before her illness, she had given him a look at his soul.

She'd taken shots he hadn't been aware of. Had she included all of them in both packages? He hoped not. The pictures of him, alone on the side of the small platform where Anna was being posed, captured too well the bleakness of his solitary life. Evan had no idea he showed that bleakness. Perhaps he didn't. Perhaps only a Wendy Fuller would recognize it, could capture it. Who was he kidding? If Anna saw these pictures, she'd recognize it. And she would never let him push her away.

And it was already all he could do to stay away.

He'd talked to Jane by telephone earlier that evening.

"When are you coming back?" she'd asked. "That Wesley puppy was here for over an hour this afternoon, hanging around, watching Anna work at the wheel. He's asked her out twice now, Evan, and if you don't get back over here, I'm afraid she's going to accept.

"She needs you. Her sister was here today. I don't know what was said, but Anna is in pain. And unless I'm very wrong, you're in pain, too. Not every woman is like Eileen, Evan. You have to know that by now. Anna Harrison is the type of woman who would love you forever."

Or until she realized she didn't really love me at all, that she just thought she did because I was the first man to treat her like the glorious woman she truly is.

He heard the massive clock in the west foyer chime the half hour and slammed the album closed. There was no sense in being late, no sense in further antagonizing his mother. She had once again begun making noises about not selling, and there was no way in hell he was going to let Riverland slip through his fingers again.

But at least, he thought as he locked the album in the desk, there was no danger that any of the dozen or so of the Claymore family's nearest and dearest who would be at Eileen's tonight would look past the facade he presented to them, no danger of any of them seeing anything he didn't want seen.

What the guests saw was a recently redecorated condominium and a recently renovated Eileen. However, only the redecoration was immediately apparent, and only the redecoration was discussed, except for more than a few comments on how well Eileen was looking, considering her recent bout with "influenza," how refreshed, how glowing.

Evan turned away from the group of people he had grown up knowing, a group that had changed little through the years, dropping a few persons, adding a few, careful always to select from only the *best*, but remaining essentially as limited and as limiting as a ghetto of medieval days—a ghetto with the gates controlled from the inside, but a ghetto all the same.

Had Reed and Vivian Harrison—he'd dragged the names of Anna's parents up from somewhere in his memory—been a part of this select group? Had her Uncle Toby been?

He spotted Tom Fairmont across the room. Tom was an infrequent visitor to Eileen's inner circle. Evan snared a drink from a tray carried by a passing waiter and moved across the room.

Tom saluted him with his wineglass. "I see you got dragged to this gathering, too. I suspected foul play when Eileen called. Now I'm sure of it. A celebration, perhaps, for averting a lawsuit?"

"Oh, hell," Evan muttered. "She wouldn't."

"Wouldn't she?"

Of course she would. Evan set his drink on the glass shelf of a nearby étagère. "Excuse me, Tom. I'm out of here."

"Evan." Tom Fairmont placed his hand on Evan's arm, stopping him. "You might want to reconsider leaving. If Eileen tells everyone tonight how brilliantly you saved Riverland, she can't very well later say you're not capable of running it, can she?"

Evan stopped, turned, and reclaimed his drink. This time, he saluted Tom. "You're as devious as I am."

"More so," Fairmont told him. "I've had more practice. Besides, your heart's not really in it."

No, Evan realized with some surprise, his heart *wasn't* in it. Not anymore. Once he could have worked this group with a finesse that had sometimes frightened him. Now he wondered why he would even have bothered. "Do the names Reed, Vivian and Toby Harrison mean anything to you?" he asked.

"Oh, yes." Fairmont sighed and took a tentative drink from his glass, then grimaced and set it aside. "How did you make the connection?"

"By accident," Evan told him. "When did you?"

"Almost immediately." He nodded toward the French doors leading to the balcony. "Let's go outside."

Outside, the night air, crisp, slightly chill, cleared the smoke from Evan's eyes and from his lungs, and carried the sounds of the party away from them. A slice of moon hung over a clear, star-studded sky and was reflected in the man-made lake that lay between the one- and two-story individual units in the complex.

Tom Fairmont led Evan to the distant end of the balcony and leaned against the railing. He took an old-fashioned gold cigarette lighter and a package of nonfiltered cigarettes from his pocket. "You didn't say anything to anyone about the Harrisons?"

"I saw no reason to. Was there a reason?"

Fairmont sighed and tucked the cigarettes back into his pocket, but he held on to the lighter, flicking the top open, closing it, worrying it. "No. There was no reason. And calling the attention of this crowd to them after all these years would only have created new gossip and eventually made things worse for both their daughters."

"Did you know them?"

"We all knew them, Evan. If you'll think back, you'll probably remember them. Your dad played golf with Reed. I played tennis with him, had even made a halfhearted attempt to marry Vivian. But I suppose I'm one of only a few people who remember they had two daughters or who actually knew Anna."

"So why doesn't Anna have any money?"

"Actually, she's better off than she would have been if Reed hadn't cut her out of the will."

"He what—?"

Tom held up a hand, silencing him. "He hid her away in his house from the day she was born until it was time for her to start school. Few of us ever saw her, and then only accidentally. He sent her to private school, away from here, and he disinherited her. Only a quick-thinking lawyer convinced him that he needed to provide for her so she wouldn't contest his will. That's when he established her trust fund. And he couldn't touch it, not even when his drinking got so bad that he finished destroying the business. And Toby couldn't touch it. Not even when his gambling got so bad that he sold all of his interest in Oakcraft Furniture to support his addiction."

"What beautiful people."

"Aren't we all, my boy? Aren't we all?"

"Evan? Tom? Are you out here?"

Evan heard his mother's voice over the suddenly louder din from the party as the doors were opened. For a moment he felt a small boy's desire to slip over the balcony railing and escape. For a moment, dragged up from long-hidden memories, he felt a small boy's thrill that his beautiful mother was calling him to a grown-up party to show him off. Anna's parents had probably been a part of one of those parties. But Anna had never been shown off. She'd been hidden away as something to be ashamed of. While Lisa—Evan didn't have to ask, he knew—Lisa had been pampered and petted and posed.

"What was their sin?" Evan asked quietly. "If alcohol and gambling and child abuse didn't get them ostracized, what finally cast them out of this illustrious circle?"

"Evan?" He heard his mother's voice coming closer in the shadows of the balcony.

"They lost their money. That's the only sin of any consequence. I thought you knew that by now, son." Fairmont snapped his lighter shut and slipped it into his pocket. "Over here, Eileen," he called softly. "We're just on our way in."

* * *

Evan left the party as soon after dinner as he could decently escape. He let himself into Jed's dark mansion, went directly to the library and settled himself in his father's chair, once again holding the album. Anna smiled up at him from every page. After the life she'd led, how in God's name could she smile? But she did. At Jane, at Lisa, at Wendy, at everyone she met. At him. And she thought she loved him. He saw it in her eyes, felt it in her touch, heard it in her voice every time he was with her.

But how would she know? How could she possibly know?

He could take advantage of her. Every instinct he had cried out for him to take what she offered, to take the warmth and joy and passion that was Anna into his life, into his heart, to take her slender, responsive body and love her until neither of them knew where one ended and the other began. To surround himself with her smile, her laugh, her talent, her wonderfully mismatched home, and to bury himself in her until neither of them was aware of the world outside, of the emptiness before they had met, of the emptiness waiting after they parted.

No. Anna's life would not be empty. Not ever again.

And Evan had to give her the opportunity to discover that.

But first, before she left his life, for her and maybe even for him, he could give her the romantic evening that Jane had tried to plan and he had ruined. He could ease her into the life she had been born to live. He could do that. And then he could let her go.

Anna stepped back from her workbench and stretched, twisting her neck and back, and then studied the wax sculpture surrounded by the paraphernalia of plaster casting. Her days had been so full with making pots and vases and bowls that she had found little time to work on it. But now the butterfly was as complete as she could make it. Now she was ready for the next critical stage in its creation, and she knew she was almost too tired to do it tonight. But she also knew there would be no more convenient time until after Christmas.

The wing bothered her. It was so fragile, so delicate. A misstep in casting, in bracing, or in pouring, and it would be destroyed. But to make it visibly stronger would destroy it just as completely, because the beauty of the sculpture lay in its delicacy, its promise.

"Anna?"

Anna looked up, distracted, and found Jane standing in the doorway, wearing a thick terry robe and holding her portable phone. "Is something wrong?" she asked quickly.

Jane shook her head, and once again Anna caught sight of that surprising pleased smile that sometimes lit Jane's eyes. "No. I don't think anything's wrong. Evan's on the phone. He wants to talk to you."

Ten

She belonged in his house.

He'd thought so when he picked her up, but the moment Anna stepped into the massive main foyer of Jed Claymore's house and he saw her surrounded by dark walnut paneling and standing beneath a converted gaslight fixture only slightly more ornate than the one hanging in her dining room, Evan knew so without a doubt.

He'd told her to dress for dinner and dancing, not knowing at the time exactly where he would take her. Her selection would have been appropriate anywhere, but never more than here.

The style of her dress was too current to have come from a vintage clothier or from Wendy Fuller's wonderful collection, and her hair was still much too short. But with her skirt gently flaring around her legs, lace the color of antique parchment at her throat, those endless tiny buttons covered with that same lace marching from her throat to her waist, and her beautiful, touchable hair combed up and away from her face in a manner that suggested one of those elaborate, upswept hairstyles, Anna looked as though she could have stepped down from one of the many oil paintings that graced the second-floor landing.

He hadn't known where to take Anna, how to give her the evening she deserved without subjecting her to stares and whispers and questions about the past. Those were all things she would someday encounter, but he didn't want them to mar his last evening with her. He'd been reluctant to bring her here, afraid she would think he was ashamed to be seen with her, afraid she would think that he, too, was hiding her away.

In desperation, he turned to Jane. He'd told himself he would never again ask anything of her for himself. But this wasn't for him, after all, it was for Anna, and with remarkable ease she had come up with the solution.

So he had programmed the compact disc player that piped music to selected rooms with Chopin and Tchaikovsky and Rachmaninoff, he'd cranked up the converted coal burner in the basement and lit fires in the downstairs fireplaces to warm rooms that hadn't been warm for years, hired a caterer to provide an elegant late supper for two, and prayed he had removed any question from her mind about his not wanting to be seen with her.

He saw delight dancing in her eyes as she looked from the foyer into the hallway, into the rooms visible from where they stood, and at the great staircase at the other end of the hall.

"This is wonderful," she told him.

"Yes," he said, feeling a little of the pride he only rarely allowed himself. "Jed did all right for himself, didn't he?"

Anna's laugh broke off as a dark-suited man, a member of the caterer's staff and butler for the night, stepped into the foyer. "May I take your cape, Miss Harrison?"

Smiling solemnly—though Evan thought he saw her lips twitch at least once—Anna handed the man her cape.

The man responded just as solemnly. "Everything you requested is ready, sir."

"Thank you, William." Taking Anna's hand, he nodded at the man and led Anna from the foyer, through the main hall and into another, smaller, but no less grand hallway.

"A butler, Evan?" she asked, mischief giving melody to her words. "Jane didn't mention a butler."

He paused, lifted her hand to his chest, and glanced at her with his best "lord of the manor" expression. Actually, he knew that expression could be daunting; he'd been told so, many times. But Anna's delight was catching. He felt his smile fighting to answer hers, and surrendered to it.

"I've not actually thought I needed one before. However, one could grow accustomed to such service, couldn't one?"

She grinned at him. "Yes, Evan, one certainly could." She squeezed his hand and looked around. "Where are you taking me? Is this by any chance a tour of the fabled and historic Claymore house?"

He shook his head. "Only a part of it, for now. Later," he said, noticing her small frown of disappointment, "I promise you a tour from boiler room to attics, if that's what you want. But for now I have something else planned." And he hoped to God he had planned it right. What if he had misjudged Anna? What if Jane had been wrong? What if, in his desire to give something to Anna, he had given her only reminders and pain?

Too late. His reservations came too late. Already he heard the music floating up from downstairs, and he knew Anna heard it, too. She turned toward him with a question in her wonderful eyes. He squeezed her hand and nodded toward a wide archway toward the end of the hall. "Through there," he said.

Through there led to a wide, carpeted stairway, leading down. Anna felt like Alice following the white rabbit as

Evan led her downward. At the base of the stairs, closed doors led to what she supposed to be the nether regions of the basement and what appeared to be an outside entrance, and a slightly worn but still-elegant hallway led in the direction from which she heard music—music that sounded different from the softly romantic classic piece piped through the upper floor, music that sounded . . . live?

"Billiard room," Evan told her as they passed a set of open double doors, and she glimpsed an antique table with net ball pockets occupying the center of the darkened room.

"Ladies' retiring room," he said, nodding to a room on the left, its doors also open to reveal graceful couches, chairs and tables, all also slightly worn, but still elegant.

"Good grief, Evan." Anna had found her voice at last. "How big is this place?"

"Big," he told her conspiratorially, "I think all those years on riverboats and in wagons must have given Jed claustrophobia. But it really isn't as big as it appears at first. And you know, this really was out in the country when he built it. There weren't a lot of social amenities available to him. He had to provide for guests."

"Sure." Anna's grin broke free. "Every comfortable country home needs several thousand feet of public rooms." She nodded to the double doors at the end of the hallway. "What's through there? The ballroom?"

"Actually. . ." Evan had begun to look a little uncomfortable, much as he had for a moment in the upstairs hall, but before Anna could explore that perception, he smiled at her and resumed his slightly irreverent tour-guide persona and led her to those doors. "Actually, yes."

"Good evening, Miss Harrison, Mr. Claymore," a young woman dressed in the same formal black as William said as she stepped from a nearby alcove. She opened the doors for them and stepped back, allowing them entrance, and Anna her first true glimpse of the nineteenth-century splendor of Jed Claymore's dream.

Light glistened from thousands of crystals in the over-head chandeliers that lined the center of the room, and from the sconces on each wall. The ceiling moldings, the chandeliers' escutcheons, the columns which supported the massive ceiling, all were deeply carved and figured. The ceiling itself bore a mural that worked its way around the room, incorporating and sometimes ignoring impediments to its path. The walls were covered with silk and mirrors, the floor with tiny hardwood parquetry and, periodically, floral-designed marquetry inlay.

Anna was so entranced by the room that several moments passed before she realized that the music was indeed live, and that it came from this room, from a raised dais in an alcove, from a small group of formally attired musicians. A magnificent old bar occupied a matching alcove, overseen by a bartender, also in black. And a young woman tended an elegantly prepared and served buffet nearby. Around the room, interspersed with the gilt chairs that must have been mandatory a hundred years or more ago, were tiny, linen-draped tables, each of them bearing a small floral arrangement and a lit candle in a silver holder.

Anna's enchantment turned to panic as she surveyed the room. Mentally she caught her hand in its instinctive, protective reach for her cheek, stopped it, but because her other hand was caught in Evan's, she could not hold it still. She clenched it in a determined fist at her side and turned to Evan.

"Oh, God, Evan..." she heard the panic in her voice, knew he had to see it in her eyes, but try as she might, she couldn't fight it down. "You haven't invited a houseful of guests, have you? I won't have to... You don't expect..."

She lost the battle with her hand; it flew to her cheek but Evan captured it in his. Releasing it, he placed his own hand over her cheek, gently, caressingly, and looked deeply into her eyes. The hesitation, even doubt, that she had thought she glimpsed earlier in his returned, but only momentarily, before he smiled at her with heartbreaking tenderness.

"Not tonight," he told her. "Someday—soon, I believe—you're going to have to face other people, face their questions...." He grinned, patting her cheek, lightening his voice, but somehow not lightening his mood. "And stun them with your beauty. But not tonight. Tonight is for us."

He led her across the room. A waiter met them at the table and held the chair for Anna. "Good evening Miss Harrison, Mr. Claymore." After she was seated he took a bottle from a waiting pedestaled wine chiller and held it toward Evan for his inspection. At Evan's nod, he removed the cork from the bottle, revealing to Anna for the first time that the wine was champagne. After the tasting ritual, he filled the crystal glass waiting at Anna's place and stepped back. "Will there be anything else, sir?" And when Evan shook his head, the man moved a discreet, out-of-hearing distance away.

Anna sipped the wine appreciatively and studied Evan over the rim of the fragile fluted glass. "Are you trying to impress me?"

Evan looked slightly confused for a moment, then gave her a rueful grin. "Until this moment, I hadn't thought so."

She wondered about the confusion and the slight wistfulness she thought she heard in his voice before she matched his grin and toasted him with her glass. "You're succeeding," she told him in a mock whisper.

Laughing, he rose from his chair and held his hand out for her. "Dance with me?"

Laughing, she set her glass on the impossible little table and rose to join him.

But their laughter stopped when he took her in his arms, when their bodies touched, when he led her in the timeless, graceful steps of the waltz. Anna had loved him before, had known it with a surety that shocked her defensive, shock-resistant heart. But after this extravagant—*perfect*—at-

tempt of his to please her, she thought that she could probably quite happily die for Evan Claymore.

And she had wanted him before, had known it with a
surety that went beyond any reason. But after this exquisite, torturous closeness, she thought she would quite probably die if they didn't follow the desire thrumming with
tantalizing thoroughness through her body to its natural
conclusion.

Later, too late for Anna's safety, for her sanity, for her
heart, William appeared in the ballroom to announce that
their supper awaited them.

As quiet as she, Evan escorted her upstairs. Two places
had been set at the cherry table in the dining room, one at
the head of the table and one immediately to the left of that,
and fresh flowers and lit candelabra stretched the length of
the center of the impressive table. No sooner had Evan
seated her and then himself than William appeared from
beyond a heavy door with wine, followed by a young woman
carrying a silver tray from which the butler served the soup
course. The two servers then left the room by way of the
same heavy door.

Anna looked at the array of crystal and silver and china
at each place setting, unerringly picked up her soupspoon,
and glanced at Evan. Her awareness of him was just as intense as it had been while she was in his arms, just as demanding, but now it was tempered by a warm burst of
affection that she felt sure had nothing to do with passion,
nothing to do with the love she felt for him.

"I think you must be crazy for doing this, Evan. I have no
idea what devious paths your mind must have wandered to
come up with this plan. But I thank you for an evening I will
never forget."

He must be crazy, Evan thought. Crazy to have imagined
he would be able to let Anna go after tonight. Crazy to think
he could get through this evening without yanking her into
his arms and carrying her up the stairs to a bed or down to

the floor to make wild and unrestrained love to her. Crazy to think that a houseful of strangers and all his good intentions could keep him from wanting to do so.

Of course he couldn't do that. And he couldn't tell her any of what he had just thought. Instead, he lifted his wine glass to hers. "Thank you."

Her awareness of him was evident, and her desire was as evident as the joy she was taking in the evening. As they finished their soup, he signaled for William and saw Anna's surprise as the butler entered, this time followed by two servers: one with a silver tray to which William removed the used service pieces, the other with a tray from which he served the second course. After pouring the wine, the butler again left them alone.

"How did he know?" Anna whispered. "Is he watching through a peephole?" She glanced around, humor dancing in her eyes, playing with the corners of her mouth, singing in her voice. "A hidden camera? Clairvoyance?"

Evan chuckled. "A bell in the floor under the Kirman."

"Oh?" Anna laughed in delight. Leaning back in her chair, she peered under the table, but he knew she saw nothing but the Oriental rug. Her expressive eyes looked at him questioningly; her dark gold brows drew together in a slight frown.

"Here," he said, pointing with his toe toward an almost invisible bump in the carpet. "It's original. I don't know if it was Jed's idea or if it was standard equipment on country mansions."

"Where?" Anna asked, reaching with her foot, then drawing back quickly. "Oh."

William entered the dining room almost immediately. "Yes, sir?"

Evan looked at Anna, who had brought her hand to her mouth and was looking for all the world like a guilty six-year-old caught sliding down the banister.

"Never mind, William," he said smoothly. "I've changed my mind."

William looked from him to Anna, but not so much as a hint of a smile marred his performance. "Very good, sir."

Evan heard a flurry of giggles, quickly stifled, from Anna the moment the door closed behind William. He glanced at her solemnly.

"Never mind, William," she said in a deep, stern voice. "I've changed my mind. Oh, you are good."

"Yes," he said, loving the laughter that animated her, admitting to himself for the first time that he had done well by giving her this evening, in this way. "Yes," he said in an equally deep, equally stern voice, "I believe I am."

She belonged in his house.

Evan thought that again as they entered the library after dinner, as Anna sat on the Chippendale sofa in front of a crackling fire in the fireplace and poured their coffee from the graceful silver coffee service William had placed there before he and the rest of the staff left for the evening.

She belonged in his house. In his bed. In his heart.

In your dreams, Claymore, he told himself.

He hadn't brought her here to seduce her. And he definitely hadn't brought her here to entangle their lives any more than they already were.

But when she handed him the delicate cup and saucer, when their fingers brushed, when he felt the awareness that flowed between them like electricity, that had flowed between them all evening, he set the cup aside, took her hand and drew her to her feet.

He touched his fingers to her lips, to the firm line of her jaw, traced the impossibly graceful line of her throat to the first of those tiny lace-covered buttons over her heart. He felt the tremor that moved through her, saw the quickened swell of her breathing.

"Is this..." her voice was as raspy, as hesitant, as he knew his would be. "Is..." She swallowed once, stepped a fraction of an inch away from his touch, and looked at him with questioning dark eyes. "Is it time for the tour, yet?"

He hurt with wanting her; he suspected that for the rest of his life, when he thought of Anna, he would hurt with wanting her. "Yes," he said, swallowing once, dying a little. "Yes. If you want."

For endless moments she stood, within his reach and yet apart from him. Her eyes were dark and luminous, her lips were gently parted but not smiling, her breathing was quick and shallow, as was outlined by the rise and fall of the lace across her breasts.

"Yes," she said finally, and he heard a resolve he couldn't begin to understand in her simple statement. "Yes. I want."

He nodded abruptly. Almost afraid to reach for her hand, afraid of his reaction to her touch, he did so anyway, taking it in his, leading her from the library.

In the hallway, she turned toward the staircase. "I want to see the portrait of your great-great-grandmother."

Evan nodded, knowing which one she meant, remembering their lighthearted banter during the photography session. He guided her upstairs to the portrait.

Anna studied it silently for a moment. "The Cherokee maiden?" she asked.

Evan shook his head. "I don't know. She could be a myth."

Jed's portrait hung next to that of his wife. It had been painted late in his life, but Evan's great-great-grandfather had still been a powerful-looking man.

"You look like him," Anna told him.

"Do you think so?" Evan asked, inordinately pleased, although he had never consciously noticed the resemblance.

Anna nodded. "You'll be a very distinguished-looking older man." She glanced down the side hallway, where numerous other portraits hung. "Who are those people?"

Evan smiled, at last released from her thrall enough to be able to do that much. "Jed and Great-great-grandma had nine children."

"Nine?" Anna asked in a shocked whisper. "She couldn't have been as prim as she looks in her portrait."

"No. Only in public, I think. I told you that..." He caught himself in time to modify his former words. "I told you that she lusted after him."

Anna turned toward him and took the step that left them only a breath apart. "Evan?" She lifted her hand to his cheek and held it there while she looked into his eyes. "Evan, *I* lust after *you.*"

He felt his breath catch in his throat, felt his heart, for more than a moment, stop. He hadn't meant to do this, but he had sent the catering staff home, leaving them alone. He hadn't meant to do this, but he had made sure he had protection for Anna. He hadn't meant to do this, but with a sense of inevitability he would not yet question, he swung her up into his arms and carried the woman he might never be able to claim as his own down the hall, to the room he had not yet claimed as his own, to the massive oak four-poster bed that had belonged to Jed Claymore.

Anna felt her world tilt as Evan lifted her into his arms, felt it right itself as he held her close to his heart and carried her down the dimly lit hallway.

She didn't believe that she had found the confidence, the nerve, to let Evan know how much she wanted him. She couldn't yet believe that he wanted her as much as she wanted him.

This will be different, she told herself. *Evan is different.*

And then she shut her mind and her heart to voices from her past.

He set her on her feet in a darkened room. Somewhere in the hall, she had lost a shoe. She kicked off the other one and felt the luxury of a thick rug beneath her feet, felt the luxury of the silk-and-wool blend of Evan's jacket beneath her hands as she braced herself against him, waiting. God, she felt as though she had always been waiting for this man.

He lifted both hands to her face, cupping it, holding it still, while they looked deep into each other's eyes, while Anna saw past the facade Evan presented to the world to a heart that was as new and yet as wounded as her own.

His hands moved from her face to her shoulders, down the lace that covered her arms and finally captured her hands, lifting them between them, palms up. Bending slightly, he kissed each palm before releasing one hand and reaching for the first of the six tiny buttons that guarded each of her wrists.

"I've wanted to do this since the moment I saw you tonight," he murmured.

Anna felt a shiver that had nothing to do with cold and everything to do with long-denied anticipation work its way through her. But Evan misinterpreted that shiver. Not releasing her hand, he turned to the fireplace. A fire had already been laid in the hearth. Taking a long match from a nearby holder, he struck it and set it to the kindling. Within moments, the kindling and then the dry wood had caught, and light flickered across the room, illuminating a massive bed. Instinctively Anna knew that this had been Jed Claymore's bed, that this had been the room where he and the prim Victorian miss created those nine children.

Evan saw where her attention had been drawn, must have guessed where her thoughts had gone. Was that hesitation she saw in him now? Was he giving her another chance to avoid the intimacy she craved with every throb of her pulse? Well, the only chance she wanted was the one waiting for her in his arms.

Smiling, she stepped closer to him. She lifted her hands to his tie, loosened it and slipped it from his collar, then moved on to the buttons of his silk shirt, feeling him standing still and tense beneath her touch. "And I have wanted to do this," she whispered huskily.

"Anna." Her name was no more than a moan as Evan caught her close against him, as his mouth settled on hers, where it belonged, as she felt his arousal and a need that was more than physical, as he lifted her again in his arms and carried her to that marvelous, wonderful, waiting bed.

The light from the fireplace played over them as Evan undid each of the tiny buttons, as he explored the silk of her thigh to find the racy little garter belt she wore beneath French-cut tap pants, as she lovingly bared the sleekness of his flank, the smoothness of his chest, to her loving ministrations and knew on seeing him that the Cherokee maiden must have been Jed's mother and not a cast-off lover.

The music of the evening played through her mind and her heart as they caressed each other, as they touched, as they teased, as they tantalized—the romance music of the classics that had pervaded the house, the lovers' music of the ballroom, all of it blended together to orchestrate and choreograph their movements, their soft whispers, their increasingly urgent demands, until finally Evan rose above her, sleek and bronzed in the darkness, lovingly gilded by the firelight.

She felt a moment's panic as he turned from her, and then a bittersweet acceptance of why he had. There would be no fear of an unwanted pregnancy this time. But then, there would have been no fear without his caution, because a child by Evan would never be unwanted by her.

He rose over her again, looking down at her, and then he lowered his head, claiming her mouth as, slowly, cautiously, he claimed her body, filling her and creating yet more needs she had never even suspected. Her breath rushed from her, and he captured it in his mouth, taking it for his own. Her hands moved wonderingly across the firm muscles of his back, down, down. She felt his restraint in the tightened muscles of his flank, heard it in the thudding of his heart, so close to hers, opened her eyes and saw it in the tight mask of his features.

"Yes, Anna," he whispered to her as he lifted his head, as he captured her head in his hands, holding it still. "Look at me. Open your eyes. Oh, God, I have to see your eyes."

And then he began moving, at first as slowly and cautiously as he had entered her, then more surely, then with a demand that her own body echoed, matched, cried out for, as eventually her voice cried out when she reached a blinding, shuddering, never-expected release.

Seconds later, she heard Evan's own harsh moan. Only then did he lower his head, collapsing against her, still a part of her, holding her while shudders and aftershocks continued to ripple through her, while the miracle of what had happened between them continued to hold her in a spell spun by wonder and a magic she had never believed existed for her.

She turned her head on the pillow and found Evan watching her. For a moment she saw the same wonder she experienced reflected in his eyes. But too soon it was gone, replaced by something she knew so well she had no need to question what it was, only what could have caused it. Because what she saw in Evan's eyes was pain—a pain so deep, so old, so intense, that it slashed through her warm euphoria and went directly to her heart.

She lifted her hand toward his cheek, but hesitated, afraid, even after all they had just experienced, to touch him.

"Evan?" she whispered.

Eleven

"Evan?"

Evan heard the hesitation in Anna's voice, saw it in the raised hand that fluttered near but did not, would not touch his cheek. Quickly he masked his emotions and caught her hand in his, securing it over his heart, and then drawing her as close against him as was humanly possible. He knew she would hear the thundering of his heart, knew she would feel the reawakening of his body, but he also knew from her untutored responses to his lovemaking that she probably wouldn't have the experience to interpret either.

He felt his breath shudder from him as he looked over her head into the darkness.

When had he convinced himself that love didn't exist?

Had he? Or had he realized only that it could never exist for him?

And when had he, bitter, cynical, and as weary as he was of all the games played in the name of love, fallen in love with Anna?

And what in the hell was he going to do now?

He was going to take her home. That was what he was going to do. He was going to get out of this bed while he was still able to do that, because what he wanted to do was make love to her again, right now, and again, and again, and never let her leave his life.

But if he did that, he would be five kinds of bastard.

Had anyone ever truly loved Anna? Now there was a possibility—a probability—that someone would. *Now* she had the opportunity to search for, to meet, that someone, to do all the things her life had previously denied her. What she didn't need was to be tied to him by gratitude or friendship or whatever sense of obligation she had created in her innocent heart.

Slowly, reluctantly, he withdrew from her, but he tightened his arms around her when she murmured a wordless protest. "Sshh," he told her. "I have to take you home. Soon. But let me hold you for a little while longer."

"Mmm..."

Again he heard her wordless comment, this time in pleasure. She stretched against him, sending fire along all his nerve endings and heaping coals on his body's already blazing need for her.

"Are you sure you're all right?" she whispered against his chest.

Evan chuckled. He didn't know where he found the strength or even the desire to give her that, but he did. "That's supposed to be my line," he told her.

"I'm fine," Anna said, moving her hand over his heart. "I'm more than fine. If I were any more fine, I'd just ooze on down and become a part of this mattress." Her voice lowered seductively, and she repeated her earlier teasing words. "Oh, you are good."

God, didn't she know what she was doing to him? Didn't she know what letting her go was doing to him? He tightened his arms around her, squeezing her against him once more before easing away from her and twisting to sit on the side of the bed. "It's indecently late. We'd better get dressed."

Anna pulled pillows behind her, pulled the coverlet up over her and leaned against the oak headboard as Evan gathered and sorted their scattered clothes, not saying anything to him as he dressed, as he donned the armor he had always found in a well-tailored suit.

Why didn't she say anything? Why did she just lie there, propped up by more pillows than any three people needed, looking at him with those huge, dark eyes of hers that for once he couldn't read.

He found his tie and looped it through his collar, standing in front of the fireplace and looking in the mirror as he knotted it with practiced skill while he watched Anna through the mirror.

Say it! he told himself. *Say something. You have to do it. Do it now. Get it over with.* But Evan knew that nothing would ever be finished about what he felt for Anna but the words he must speak.

"I'll be going back to Virginia in the next day or so," he said.

Her voice sounded calm. Almost too calm. "How long will you be gone?"

"I don't know. Eileen is making reluctant noises about selling Riverland, and this whole process has taken so long the rest of the business is beginning to need attention."

"She will sell her interest to you, won't she?"

Still watching her in the mirror, Evan also saw his own reflection, saw how it hardened. "Yes. Nothing can keep me from getting her out. I won't let it."

"I see."

Her voice, small, hesitant, subdued, twisted his heart. He turned to face her, but he knew he couldn't let himself touch her again. "Anna, you don't think—"

"That our relatives were right in their assessment of your motives? No, Evan." She shook her head, slowly, sadly, lost among the pillows, a fragile treasure dwarfed by the massive bed. "I don't think that at all."

He felt some of the tension ease from his shoulders, from his heart, and turned back to the mirror, to the task of tying his tie, to the task of freeing Anna Harrison from any obligation she felt toward him.

"I may be gone for some time," he said. "You'll be all right, won't you?"

"I've always been able to take care of myself."

"I know. But your life has changed, Anna." He dredged up a smile for her reflection in the mirror and watched her nod. "You must know that it's going to change even more. Jane tells me you've already acquired a suitor."

"Wesley," Anna said, grimacing.

"There will be others. Many others, Anna."

"Are you telling me you want me to see other men?"

Evan heard deadly calm in Anna's voice. *No!* he wanted to cry. *You belong to me!* But he didn't. "It's inevitable," he said instead. "You're lovely. You're talented."

"Are you telling me . . ." she asked, still calm, too calm, and now her glorious eyes were not only unreadable but expressionless, a lusterless, opaque, dark armor shielding her soul as they must have countless times in the past. But never from him. Never before from him. "Are you telling me that you don't want to see me again, that this wonderful, perfect evening was your way of . . . of saying goodbye?"

He couldn't meet her eyes, either directly or in the mirror. He didn't want to answer her question. Phrased that way, his motives seemed so cold, so unfeeling. If she only knew . . . For the first time in years, he was truly feeling something. And not for the first time, but this time certainly for the last time, feeling, loving, caring, brought him nothing but the pain and futility of feeling . . . loving . . . caring. . . .

The evening had been wonderful, more than he'd ever suspected it could be, and it had been perfect, more than Anna would ever realize. And it had been, had to be, his way of saying goodbye. He sighed once, then lifted his head and turned to face her. "Yes, Anna," he told her, "it was."

This time will be different, Anna had told herself. *Evan is different.*

Well, she supposed he was different. The only other time she had surrendered her heart and body to a man, he hadn't bothered to tell her he wouldn't see her again. After weeks of wooing her, after raising her hopes about love and marriage and babies and finally taking the gift of herself, he had dropped her off at the dorm without a word of goodbye. He just hadn't been around while she suffered through the confusion of being dropped by him, while she went through the panic of thinking she might be carrying his child. Only weeks later had the rumors caught up with even her, and she had trapped him in a corner in the student union.

"A *bet,*" she'd accused him in cold fury. "You made love with me because you bet your fraternity brothers you could?"

She knew he wanted to push past her, but he couldn't without causing the scene her quietly spoken words had not yet created.

"Wrong, Anna," he said. "I had sex with you because my fraternity brothers bet me I *wouldn't.*"

She hadn't cried over Brad; she wouldn't cry over Evan. At least he'd been honest with her. He'd given her more than anyone else ever had. He just didn't want what she had to offer him. She gathered her shattered dignity around her, then reached across the bed and gathered the small pile of her clothes to her, too. "Did Jed's interpretation of luxury include a bathroom in this chamber, or do I have to wander around this mausoleum looking for one?"

* * *

The sky had barely begun to lighten, the birds to awaken, when they arrived in the parking space behind Anna's building. She reached for the door handle, but Evan stopped her with a sharp glance. She waited in the car for him to round it, for him to open the door for her. He walked her to the back stairs, but she was unwilling to take him upstairs with her, unable to remain in his sight one second longer than was absolutely necessary.

Anna opened the back door to her building and stepped inside. She turned to look at Evan. There was nothing more to be said, so she stared at him silently for a moment before closing the door on him, before closing the door on yet another painful chapter of her life.

She walked up the narrow back stairs as quietly as possible, not wanting to awaken Jane. But she met Jane coming into the kitchen from the hallway just as she entered from the service stairs.

"I'm sorry," Jane said, smiling sleepily. "I didn't know you were home." She looked at Anna, had to notice that she still wore the same clothes she had the night before, and then glanced around the kitchen. "Is Evan here?"

"No."

"Oh." Jane yawned and began the efficient preparation of coffee. "Will he be coming by later this morning?"

"No."

Jane turned slowly, studying Anna. "What's wrong?"

Anna clasped her hands, rubbing together palms that only hours before Evan had kissed. "Evan is leaving for Virginia in a day or two. He doesn't know when he will return. I don't believe he knows *if* he will return."

"That stupid, stubborn, hardheaded— And you're just going to let him go? Call him, Anna. Or go to him. Don't just let him walk away."

"I have never in my life begged for love," Anna cried. She reached out, clasping the door facing, and forced control into her voice. "Sometimes I had to fight to keep from begging, but I never begged. I don't intend to start now."

"Anna—"

"Evan told me once that he could see everything I thought, everything I felt, in my eyes. He asked me if no one else had ever looked closely enough to see. Until him, no one had. Only him. And he…he apparently didn't like what he saw."

She released the door facing and straightened to her full, fragile height. "Evan won't be coming back, Jane. If that makes a difference to you, if you have to change your plans, or make a choice between us, or leave, I want you to do it now. I think I have about enough strength left to withstand one more major loss, but I'm not sure." Anna felt tears fighting their way into her eyes, into her voice. "And I'm not sure how much longer that strength will last."

Evan let himself into Jed's house through the side hallway, shook the droplets of chill spitting rain from his overcoat and tossed the coat over the nearest chair. He'd stayed in Virginia a month the first time, returned to Fort Smith for a week but found it just as hellishly lonely as Norfolk, and returned to the East Coast for another week before surrendering to the knowledge that anywhere he went was going to be as lonely as any other place. He'd returned then to Jed's house, because at least there he had memories.

Evan was greeted in the library by the scents of lemon oil and fresh flowers, and he looked around in surprise. He'd seen evidence of Jane Mudge at work over the weeks, but in all that time he had not been greeted by these scents, as he had been in the first few weeks after her return.

He also had not been greeted by an enormous Christmas tree decorated with Victorian ornaments, such as the one that dominated the corner of the room, or by the faint sound of music coming from somewhere in the house. He followed the music upstairs, to the servants' quarters in the rear, and found Jane Mudge unpacking a small suitcase in the housekeeper's suite.

"What are you doing here?"

She looked up at him, distracted, not bothering to smile. "I work here. Have you forgotten?"

"No, but sometimes I wonder if *you* have."

Usually Jane managed to tease him out of his ill humor, but today she slammed the lid on her suitcase and turned with firm determination to face him. "Are you dissatisfied with my work?"

He shook his head. "No, Jane. You know I'm not. I'm just surprised to see you here. Why have you left Anna?"

"Her sister is moving home today, and—"

"So you just walked off and left her to deal with her alone. But you're very good at that, aren't you? Walking away from someone who needs you?"

"No better than *you*, Evan," Jane said with quiet dignity. "No better than you. Besides my abandonment, however, I do have another reason for being here," she told him, smiling brittlely. "The plasterers will be here at seven in the morning to begin the repairs to the third-floor hall. If you would rather deal with them yourself, I'll be happy to leave you to it."

She had never had to raise her voice to put him in his place. Even when he was a child, one of his harshest punishments had been knowing he'd disappointed Jane. Evan knew that nothing he had done then had disappointed her nearly so much as his words in this brief confrontation, but for the life of him, he didn't know what he had said, apart from reminding her of the truth of her actions, that had tightened her mouth and clouded her eyes.

"No," he said. "You're right, of course, to be here. I'm sorry I intruded on you."

* * *

"You're going out with Wesley?"

Lisa confronted Anna in the showroom, arms crossed, frown firmly in place.

"Look," Anna told her, "I'm sorry. I didn't know you would be moving back today. I accepted his invitation a week ago, and I haven't been able to get in touch with him to cancel. I told him I couldn't make a late evening of it." Anna hesitated, but there was no good way to say what she had to say to her sister. "Tonight, Lisa, we have to talk. I'll be home early, I promise."

"You're going out with Wesley. You're going out with a man who promised to love me until his dying breath? Have you decided you have to take over that part of my life, too?"

Anna sighed. She should have known. Or should she have? Wesley might have promised to love Lisa—God knew, enough men seemed to have made that promise—or Lisa might just be saying that because lately her sister had seemed to take great delight in spoiling any small pleasure Anna found. Although this date tonight promised to be no pleasure. Pleasure would be for everyone to leave her alone with her wax and her plaster and her memories; pleasure would be for the pain of losing Evan finally to dull to something as inconsequential as a migraine headache or a massive heart attack. Tonight promised to be merely an obligation that she had finally been badgered into accepting because she had no strength left with which to fight. Evan wanted her to go out with other men. Well, tonight she would begin.

"Tonight, Lisa," Anna said with weary resignation. "I expect you to be here when I return."

Eileen arrived unexpected and unannounced, catching Evan in the library with a bottle of cold beer and a thick sandwich he had prepared for himself and carried to his desk on a paper towel. He had heard the faint strains of Jane's music while in the kitchen, but she had not come down-

stairs to offer to prepare supper, and he had not gone upstairs with an offer to share what he had prepared.

Eileen glanced around the room appreciatively—perhaps
she was going through an antiques phase—and glared at his
sandwich and beer.

"Really, Evan, I taught you better manners than that.
With all the china and crystal in this house, surely you could
have found something to serve that disgusting concoction
on."

He raised his bottle to her, but did not rise to greet her, did
not hold her chair for her, did not apologize for his dinner
or his manners. "What brings you out on this dismal evening, Eileen?" *What do you want from me now? And what
are you going to hold out as temptation to make sure you get
it?*

"An invitation to my Christmas party," she said, giving
him a bright smile, "and an opportunity to talk to my only
son. You really have made yourself scarce, Evan. I've
missed you."

Interesting, Evan thought. Usually Eileen was much more
direct.

"Then how fortunate you had this evening free," he said
pleasantly, "because I'll probably make myself scarce the
night of the party, too. You know how I hate those crushes."

"Evan, I've been talking to Tom Fairmont...."

Here it comes. What devious...

"We have just a few more details to iron out before I'll be
ready to sign the final papers."

...twisted, diabolical...

"I've asked Margo to visit with me over the holidays."

Damnation!

"No," he said, still pleasant, still smiling, as he tipped his
bottle back and drank deeply.

"Hear me out. I have no idea what your little spat was
about—"

"It was about my not wanting her anywhere near me, Eileen. It was about my not wanting to live the kind of life she lives. It was about my not wanting to associate myself with the standards she accepts as normal."

"But I talked with her at length, and we've agreed that if you will be reasonable with her settlement in the prenuptial agreement, she will forgive you for those horrible, harsh things you said to her."

"Harsh?" Obviously, Eileen wouldn't listen, but Evan felt compelled to say this. "I never thought 'goodbye' to be particularly harsh, but perhaps 'I never want to see you again' might be construed that way. Possibly even, 'We have absolutely nothing in common' might be."

"But, darling boy, you do have. This is what I couldn't understand about your totally incomprehensible interlude with this nothing little person in Van Buren. And neither, fortunately, could Margo. Thank God you've come to your senses about *her*."

Evan clutched the neck of the beer bottle with one hand, the arm of his chair with the other. Eileen and Margo had apparently had quite a conference, dissecting him, picking apart Anna. Come to his senses, had he? Not yet. Not where Anna was concerned. Maybe not ever.

"Cut to the chase, Eileen," he said wearily. "I've had a hell of a long day already, and I don't intend for it to last much longer."

"What language. Very well, Evan. Margo and I have decided that we can announce your engagement at the Christmas party. If her parents and I begin right now, we should be able to pull off a truly spectacular wedding by the end of January."

None of this surprised him. It should have. And it should have hurt like hell. But somewhere along the way he had escaped from his mother's ability to cause him pain. Maybe because he was already in so much pain that he had caused himself that there was no room for more.

"And?" he asked.

"Whatever do you mean?"

"And the rest of it? What happens after Margo and I return from . . . from what? A monthlong honeymoon in the Bahamas perhaps?"

"Why, that would be nice," Eileen said. "Much better than what she and I discussed. I'm so glad you're being reasonable, Evan."

"The rest of it, Eileen," he said, all patience gone. "What's the carrot? What's the enticement? What will you hold over my head this time to make sure I do what you want?"

Eileen smiled contentedly at him and settled back in her chair. "Why, Riverland, dear. *When* you return from your honeymoon with Margo, and only then, I will sign the final sale papers."

He was out of his chair, halfway around the desk, when he realized he had risen. He had no idea what he intended, but a soft, shocked gasp from the doorway stopped him. He looked up to see Jane standing there, holding a vase that was masculine enough to fit in this library, delicate enough to be the work of only one potter.

"I'm sorry," Jane said, placing the vase on the nearest table. "I should have given you this earlier. I didn't realize you weren't alone." Casting one brief, pained look at Eileen, she turned and fled from the room.

"What is that woman doing in my house?" Eileen leaped from the chair, her face flushed, her breathing rapid. "I want her out of here! This instant!"

Evan glanced from his mother, whom he remembered as never, ever, losing her poise, to the empty doorway from which Jane, who never backed down from anyone, had fled.

"It's *my* house, Mother. And Jane works for me."

"You're harboring her? My own son is actually harboring that woman, after all I had to do to get rid of her? How dare you?"

She had gotten rid of Jane? Jane hadn't left voluntarily? Evan returned to his chair, leaning back and closing his eyes as fragments of his childhood tried to float to the surface of his memory.

"Answer me, Evan! How dare you do this?"

He ought to take advantage of Eileen's loss of control; he might not have another opportunity. But suddenly he was so tired of manipulation and game-playing and lies.

He sighed and rubbed at a beginning headache before he faced his mother. "I dare do it the same way I dare tell you that there is no way in hell I will ever marry Margo!"

"Then there's no way in hell I'll ever sell you Riverland Trucking."

"I don't care, Eileen. For the first time in my life, there is nothing I want from you, nothing you can promise to give me and then withhold if I don't act as you want me to. I'm thirty-five years old. If you were ever going to love me, you would have done so before now. And I don't have to buy Riverland from you. It just dawned on me. After months of doing my damnedest to save the company from your incompetence. I don't have to buy it. My pride might take a beating, but all I have to do is pull myself and my crew out and wait for your cast of idiots to finish driving a once-thriving business into bankruptcy court."

"I won't let you talk to me this way—"

"You let yourself in, Eileen, so I'm sure you know your way out."

"And I won't let you drive me out of a home that is as much mine as it is yours."

He shook his head. One childhood memory in particular had floated to the surface of his mind, a memory of another time when Eileen had lost her control, had confronted and accused Jane.

"No, it isn't. Dad left it to me, remember? And I think I finally understand why. While I'm shredding my dignity groveling for our family's business in bankruptcy court, do you want me to share that understanding with a few of our dearest friends?''

Eileen paled. "You wouldn't."

"Try manipulating me one more time and find out."

Evan didn't like himself very much when Eileen left. He wondered if he ever would, if there was anything he could do to right an old and vicious wrong and heal the wound he had so unthinkingly deepened.

He found Jane sitting on her bed by her open suitcase.

"She fired you didn't she?" he asked, sharing with her the fragments of his belated memory.

Jane nodded.

"And then she blackballed you so that you couldn't find work in the area."

Again she nodded.

"She accused you of being in love with my father."

Jane looked at him.

"Were you?"

"Evan, it was a long time ago. What difference does it make now?"

"Were you in love with him?"

"Yes."

"You didn't tell him about her affairs, did you?"

"What good would that have done?"

"Was he in love with you?"

Jane lowered her head, refusing to meet his eyes. "It was never discussed."

"But that wasn't the reason she fired you."

"No. No, I made the mistake of trying to tell her how to raise you. I argued against sending you away to school."

"Why did you come back now?"

"I promised your father I'd look after you."

"Jane." His voice softened. She had to know how important this was to him. "Why did you come back?"

She looked at him through eyes shimmering with tears. "Because you were the son I never had. Because when I was forced to leave you, I felt like a part of me had been ripped away."

Evan sat down on the edge of the bed and dropped his hand onto the empty suitcase between them. "Why? Why didn't you say something years ago? Months ago? Even to-night?"

"What? What could I have told you that would have made any difference?"

"That you loved me. That you didn't walk away because you didn't love me."

The tears streamed down Jane's cheeks. "Would it have made any difference?" she asked. "Would you have be-lieved my words, any more than you believed my actions?"

He stood up and slapped his hand against the bedpost. "You don't need this job, do you?"

Jane shook her head. "No, Evan. I'm not here because I need your money."

"Good," he said, sighing. "Because you're fired. And you might as well go ahead and finish packing that suit-case."

"What—?"

"Oh, God, no, Jane," he said, realizing how his words must have sounded. He sank down beside her, holding her against him and resting his chin on her head. "I'm not sending you away, I'm moving you. Family and guests stay in the front of the house."

"And...and which am I?"

"That's up to you. But considering how this family has treated you over the years, you might want to take some time to make your decision."

Downstairs, Evan found the vase Jane had brought him from Anna and carried it to the desk. He held it in his hands, absorbing the essence of Anna that still clung to it.

He could call her. He could thank her for the vase. He could make sure she was all right, that her sister was not causing her more grief than she could bear.

Weeks of not hearing her voice had not dulled the pain of not hearing it. What harm could one call do?

God! Couldn't he stop the lies—at least the ones he told himself? He loved her. He wanted to hear her voice because each day without her he died a little more, drew into himself a little more, became even more the kind of man who couldn't see past himself to the pain of someone as important to him as Jane was.

For a while, with Anna, he had felt himself thawing, felt himself healing.

He needed her. If she never truly needed him, he needed her. And not just her voice on the telephone. He needed her touch. He needed to look into her eyes and know that he hadn't hurt her beyond even her seemingly fathomless well of forgiveness. And if he had—God, if he had—he had to try to do something to heal *her*.

Twelve

Anna had the taxi drop her off two blocks down the street from her shop. The street and the shops were well lit and hung with holiday decorations, as was her showroom, but she paid little attention to them as she began her reluctant climb up the hill. She needed the privacy; she needed the walk and the night air to clear her twisted thoughts and to prepare for the confrontation she would have at home.

She still couldn't believe she had found the courage to walk out on Wesley, his wandering hands and his slick innuendo, in the middle of dinner in a crowded, popular restaurant. She couldn't help smiling at the thought. Wesley hadn't been able to believe it, either.

Her smile faded. Wesley was a mistake, totally unsuited to her in interest and temperament and in basic character. But what if he hadn't been? What if he had been a perfectly acceptable man? What if he had taken her on a perfectly acceptable date? Would she still have been tortured by memories of Evan? Would she still have compared the evening to the one—the *only*—real date she had shared with Evan, and found it lacking?

Yes, she would have.

And she probably always would.

Why had Evan shown her such tenderness, such concern, such passion, if he had intended all along to say goodbye?

She felt her hand on her cheek and left it there, digging her fingertips into the now-perfect skin. The birthmark had been so much a part of her that she sometimes forgot it no longer visibly marked her. And she sometimes forgot that simply removing it had not automatically made her the kind of woman others could love.

Had not made her the kind of woman Evan could love.

She stopped for a changing traffic light, and a car pulled up to the curb. She recognized the owner of the coffee shop a couple of blocks over about the same time the woman recognized her and rolled down her window. "Hi there. Do you need a lift up to your place?"

Anna shook her head. "No thanks. I'm . . . I'm window-shopping."

The woman grinned, waved, and drove off when her light changed to green.

Anna shivered and turned to look in the nearest window while waiting for the mist to clear from her eyes. Window-shopping. Was that what Evan had been doing?

No, he hadn't loved her, but she couldn't credit him with motives as frivolous as that—or as devious as those her sister had tried to attribute to him. The truth was probably that he had been thrown together with her by accident and had become embroiled in her life by his strong sense of responsibility and a hefty dose of misplaced guilt.

She honestly believed he had tried not to hurt her. Thank God, she hadn't told him she loved him. She cringed every time she thought of how blatantly she had exposed her

hopeless and naive affection. She could only be thankful
that she hadn't burdened him with the words, too.

Words.

She wasn't surprised he'd had trouble finding the words
to free himself from what he had to have seen as her un-
healthy dependence on him.

Because she was having the same kind of trouble finding
the words to end another dependency, one that she was almost totally responsible for creating, and one that was well
on its way to ruining a young life.

And that was what she was supposed to be thinking about
on this walk, because when she got home she was going to
have to know what to say.

She saw Lisa's little red car parked on the street, half way
down the block from her shop and frowned. She knew Lisa
had parked in the rear earlier, knew she hated the incon-
venience of the deadbolt mechanism on the front doors,
knew that normally her sister wouldn't walk an extra five
feet unless it was absolutely necessary, let alone more than
fifty.

She glanced in the car and saw a jumble of clothes and a
suitcase, as well as an open box of her pottery—not packed,
just stuffed in the box as though grabbed off her shelves.
She closed her eyes against a wave of sorrow and wondered
for a moment if she could just leave, if she could just take
herself to the home of one of her neighbors until after Lisa
had done whatever it was she was now doing, until Lisa had
fled from the confrontation that she apparently wanted even
less than Anna did.

But she couldn't.

She'd turned her head too many times, avoided the inevitable so often that the inevitable had become almost the
impossible.

Her front door was locked. She twisted her key in each of
the two locks and opened the door on the right. The bell
wired to the door didn't sound. Anna frowned and looked

around the night- and Christmas-lit showroom. The bell had been unplugged; a few blank spaces had appeared on her shelves. Nothing else looked disturbed. She turned to lock the door behind her, but a noise from within the building stopped her.

Leaving her keys hanging in the door lock, Anna went through the showroom to the long hallway leading to the back of the building. A dim light glowed from the room she used as a sometime office. The noises of a quiet and systematic search came from there.

She was afraid. But not of an intruder.

Anna stepped quietly into the room. Lisa was bent over, prowling through a bottom desk drawer, while the empty drawer from the cash register gaped open on the desk's top.

"I had a vault installed for any money I have to keep on the premises," Anna said softly.

"Anna!"

Lisa jerked upright and whirled to face her.

"I could tell you I did it because I was afraid of burglars," Anna continued. "But we both know why I had to start locking the money away, don't we?"

"I wasn't..."

Anna glanced pointedly at the open cash drawer, and Lisa fell silent.

"Lisa," Anna said, the weight of her disappointment slowing her words, "you never had to steal from me."

"Steal from you? *Steal* from *you?* Yes, I guess you would call it that. But what you did to me wasn't stealing. You just got your hands on my trust fund, squeezed it tight and refused to let go."

Anna had expected denial, perhaps even tears and an undisguised play for sympathy, but she had never expected to hear accusation from her sister.

"You've always hated me, haven't you, Anna? Always been jealous of me. I can remember when Mama and Daddy were still alive. I used to see you peeking around the corners, and I knew even then that you resented me because they loved me and not you.

"Then later, when I started dating, I knew that you envied every boy that smiled at me. Is that why you couldn't let Uncle Toby be my guardian? So you could tell me, 'No, Lisa, you can't go out with that one, or this one?' Is that why you couldn't wait to be appointed trustee? So you could make damn sure that I didn't have enough to live on without having to come crawling to you between checks and justify what I bought?"

Too late. Anna knew she had waited too late, had prolonged a situation that ought never to have started, and her only defense was that she hadn't wanted to hurt Lisa's pride. But how had she earned such venom?

"I thought your quarterly payments were...were at least adequate for your needs," she said quietly.

"Adequate? Maybe for *you*. There wasn't any point in your buying decent clothes or a car fit to be seen in. But you're doing that now, aren't you? You got what you wanted out of that accident—to hell with me or my needs— and now *you* of all people, are trying to take my boyfriends away from me, too!"

"Lisa, I've never taken anything away from you. If you'll stop and think, you'll know that's true. I've never asked anything of you except that you be the best person you can be."

"Right," Lisa said. "And you were the one who decided what that *best* was. But no more, Anna. I want you off my trust fund. If you don't resign, I'm going to have you removed."

Anna walked into the room and dropped into a chair in front of the desk, sighing, dying a little. "I can't do that. And neither can you."

"Just watch, sister mine. You'll be lucky if I don't press charges against you for misappropriation of my money."

"You don't have any money!" The words erupted from her before Anna could even consider recalling them.

Lisa stared at her in shocked silence. "You're lying. Daddy told me . . . he told me that I was the only daughter he wanted or needed. He told me he'd already given you all you'd ever need and he was leaving everything to me."

Anna leaned her head back against the chair and massaged throbbing temples. Her father had told her the same thing. The only new pain in Lisa's words came from her sister's need to hurt her. "Lisa, by the time our parents died, *everything* was a pile of debts."

"I don't believe you. Uncle Toby—"

"Uncle Toby was a dear, irresponsible man with a passion for fine wood and for any kind of wager, and he died of an illness that drained away what few resources those two passions had left him."

"But my trust fund . . ."

Anna shook her head.

"I have a trust officer at the bank. I get quarterly statements."

"I wanted to give you your pride. I wanted to give you independence. I'm sorry. Apparently I failed."

"So every dime I get comes from . . . from you?" Lisa fell silent while she tried to absorb that unwanted knowledge. "And I suppose that's going to quit now?"

"No," Anna said. "It's not going to quit. But it is going to change. I was going to tell you that tonight." She laughed, abruptly, bitterly. "Not quite in this way. And maybe not quite this truthfully.

"You have to do something with your life, Lisa. You can't go on like you have, using people, depending on your beauty to ease your way through any situation. The world owes you nothing—"

"And I suppose the rest of that is that you don't, either."

"I'm family, Lisa. And I was your guardian. I don't know anymore what I owe you, but what I have to give you is the love you don't seem to want. And a chance at life. I've talked to the bank about revising your income on the condition that you enroll in college next semester and that you move into student housing. I don't care what you study, so long as it leads to a degree in a reasonable length of time. I don't care what career you choose, so long as you pursue it with diligence and, I hope, with some pleasure."

"Is that all?"

Anna drew a deep breath. "No," she said, trying to remember all the reassurances of the counselor she had consulted, and praying she wasn't driving Lisa completely away. "You won't believe this now, Lisa. But I'm doing this for you own good."

Lisa's sharp crack of laughter was like a slap across her face. "Don't lie to me about your motives. You're doing this because you *can* do it. You're doing it because you're a bitter, frustrated woman, and I'm the only thing handy to take that frustration out on. I told you Claymore was only using you, but you wouldn't believe me. Now he's gone. Big surprise. You didn't really think you could hold on to someone like him, did you, Anna? Good Lord, a loser like Wesley had you home by ten o'clock.

"And do you know why? Because taking that mark off your face didn't change you one bit. You'll never be a beautiful woman, because you don't know how to be. There is much more to beauty than your appearance. There's an attitude, a talent, a completely different way of grabbing what you want from life. Things that a charity surgery can't give you."

"Then I am truly blessed, aren't I?" Anna said, rising to her feet, at last realizing that she didn't have to endure Lisa's abuse any more than she had endured Wesley's groping, at last realizing that continuing to endure it was helping neither her nor her sister.

"I don't know what you mean."

"I don't suppose you would, Lisa. But from what I've seen of what you must consider true beauty, I want nothing to do with it. And I want nothing more to do with helping you ruin your life. It's apparent from the condition of your car that you don't plan to stay here tonight, so I'd like to lock up and go to bed. I'd also like to have your keys before you leave. I don't expect you to unload my pottery tonight. You can bring it back tomorrow. You have a week to consider my offer."

"Just like that."

Anna nodded. "Just like that. I'm tired, Lisa. I'm tired of trying to reach you. I'm tired of being hurt by your callousness. And I'm physically tired. The keys, please."

Anna held out her hand, and Lisa threw the keys into it. She closed her fist over them, closed her eyes to the sight of her sister's angry face, closed her ears to the sounds of Lisa leaving, closed her heart to the emptiness of her home and her life.

"She's wrong, you know."

Anna's eyes flew open, and she turned toward the hallway, toward a voice she had thought never to hear again. *God, no,* she prayed. *Please. I can't handle this now. I don't have the strength to pretend I don't care.*

Evan stood half in shadow across the darkened hall, and from where he stood he could have seen everything, heard everything that took place.

"You... Have you been there long?" she asked.

"Long enough. I didn't think I should intrude. Am I intruding, Anna?"

Apparently she no longer had the strength to stand, either. Her knees buckled, and she crumpled onto the edge of the chair. "No. You could never intrude."

"Thank God for that."

He stepped into the room and placed another set of keys on the desk. "You left these in the front door."

She looked up at him in question, and he smiled hesitantly, almost apologetically. "I was driving around, trying to drag up the courage to ring your night bell, when I saw you enter the shop."

"Why?" she asked. "Why are you here? And why would you need courage?"

"I was jealous."

She looked up at him, and he nodded. "It's true. After all my rationalization about how I had to free you to explore this new world of yours, I learned that I couldn't do that. I didn't know what I'd find when I got here, whether you'd even be here—or who would be with you.

"I telephoned," he said, sitting on the edge of the desk, so close to her they almost touched. "Lisa told me you had a date."

"Oh, Evan."

"Sshh . . . Let me say this, please, while I still can. I knew very soon after I met you that you thought you loved me."

Anna felt her face flame with color and twisted her head away from him, but he captured her chin in his fingers and tilted her face toward him. "I refused to accept that you really did. I decided that it had to be gratitude or a sense of obligation, and that to be fair to you I had to free you from that obligation."

She took a breath to speak, but he lifted a finger to her lips and shook his head.

"I decided you were like that butterfly of yours," he continued, "that you had to have the opportunity to try your beautiful new wings, that you had to have the opportunity to sample the nectar from all those flowers that had been closed to you in the past. I decided that if I took all I truly needed from you, I would destroy you and everything you thought you felt for me.

"I was being so magnanimous," he told her, "so altruistic in letting you go."

And killing me in the process, she wanted to cry, but his hand on her jaw, his finger on her lips, the tension she felt in him through that point of contact, kept her silent. *Don't you know that I don't just* think *I love you? Don't you know that you gave me much more than you ever took?*

"And then I realized I was not acting out of any benevolent motives—I was acting out of fear. I wasn't just afraid that you *didn't* love me—I was afraid that you *couldn't* love me. That no one could."

"Evan—"

"And I realized that I didn't want you trying those new wings of yours for anyone but me. I realized that you are a rare and beautiful person—inside and—" he moved his fingers across her cheek "—outside." His voice deepened; his eyes glinted with suspicious moisture. "I don't know if I would have been able to see behind the disguise nature gave you, Anna, if we hadn't had our time together while you were still bandaged. I hope I would have, but I can't be positive. For that I'm more sorry than you can ever imagine. I've seen the depth of your ability to love, Anna, and if by pushing you away I've destroyed the chance that you might someday truly love me, I might as well condemn myself to hell right now.

"What do you say?" he asked, and she saw in his eyes the reflection of a heart as wounded and fragile as her own. "I wanted to free you so you could fall in love. Do you think you could fall in love with me?"

She felt tears raining down her cheeks. This beautiful, caring man loved her. This beautiful, caring man thought that she didn't—that she *couldn't*—love him. "Evan—"

"I promise you, Anna, no one else will ever love you as much as I do. No one else will ever treasure you as much as I do. No one else will ever need you as much as I do.

"I didn't believe in love until I met you, sweet, sweet Anna. You taught me that I can give love. Will you let me give you mine?"

Anna pushed his hand away from her chin and surged to her feet, sliding her arms around his chest and burrowing against him while tears and sobs broke from her. "Evan, until you, no one ever—"

"Sshh . . . You don't have to cry."

"No one ever let me cry before. No one ever held me. No one ever comforted me." She sniffed and chuckled. "No one ever wanted my picture before. Or gave me a fairy-tale evening. Or made sure everyone in the house, from the butler to the busboy, knew who I was and who I was with. No one ever made such exquisite love to me."

"I know, Anna. God help me, I know. And I don't want you to confuse what you feel about that with love."

"You wonderful, innocent man. Don't you know that until you, no one ever saw who I really am, and that I never thought anyone could love me, either? Don't you know that what I feel is love, and that what you have done would make any woman fall in love with you?"

No, he didn't. She felt the tension in his arms as he held her and knew she had to find words to convince him. Or actions. Because so much of the love he now told her he wanted to give her, he had already shown her—exquisitely, as she had just reminded him.

"Evan," she murmured, turning in his arms, reaching for him with her heart, until no more than a whisper separated them. "Evan," she whispered.

She heard him moan shakily just before their lips met in an agony of need that neither tried to hide, before he lost the awesome control that had held his arms tense and unresponsive at his sides and grasped her as though she were the only thing standing between him and a fate too awful to contemplate.

And maybe she was, Anna realized. Just as he was for her.

But then there was no more time for thought. She was with Evan again, as she had never truly hoped to be. Her heart exulted in his love, and all the nerve endings in her body sprang to life.

Somehow, they found their way upstairs in the bedroom where she had once convinced herself she could be content alone. Had she been lying to herself all her life until this night?

Soft light from one lamp cast an amber glow across the elaborate metal bed with its blatantly romantic comforter and pillows and across the sharp planes of Evan's cheek. He lifted a gentle hand to her face and brushed at the spiky wetness of her lashes, at the tender, damp flesh of her cheek. She smiled at him, and her smile was as tentative as his touch. This was new territory they covered tonight, similar yet so different from their night at Evan's house, because now she didn't have to hide her love from him, didn't have to protect herself from the hurt of rejection, didn't have to restrain herself from touching him the way she wanted.

She felt her smile grow bolder, as she herself did. Lifting her hands to Evan's chest, she undid one button on his shirt, then another.

"Anna..."

She heard the desire in Evan's choked whisper. "Yes?" she asked, sliding her fingers inside his shirt, finding warm bronzed skin that was so much more alive, so much warmer and responsive than the bronze she had once imagined sculpting.

"Oh, yes," he said, catching her hand with his and holding it still, over his heart. "Definitely yes."

Her chuckle surprised her. She had never truly believed that loving could be fun—breathtaking, overpowering, catching her in a sensual spell that exceeded anything she had ever imagined, and yet playful. Grinning, she stepped from her shoes and gave Evan a little push backward, toward the bed.

The high mattress caught him behind the knees. After one startled, disbelieving glance at her, he laughed, too, triumphantly. Holding her protectively in his arms, he twisted with her, taking them both down into the luxurious softness of Anna's bed.

She felt his lips moving over her cheek, felt the gentle foray of his tongue at the shell of her ear, felt the tender caress of his breath as he murmured her name.

"I thought I'd never be able to be with you like this again."

His words echoed her own fears and she couldn't allow them to intrude.

"Sshh," she said softly. "Not now. Now, just love me Evan, and let me love you."

"Like this?" he asked, lifting his hand to cup her breast, to rub his thumb over her already aching and sensitive nipple. She felt the tug of her response throughout her body, felt already sensitized nerves sizzle and sing with a need that only Evan had ever been able to ignite and satisfy.

"Hmmm... something like that," she whispered as his other hand began working with the buttons of her dress. "Oh, yes," she said. "I do believe you've got the right idea."

Oh lord, did he ever have the right idea. Her breath caught as she felt his lips on the soft flesh of her breast, felt the hot, wet caress of his mouth.

"Let me help," she murmured, reaching again for the buttons of his shirt, for the warmth of his chest, needing to feel him against her with nothing between them. But she was very much afraid she wouldn't be able to help, afraid that the sensations would swamp her before she could begin to show Evan how much he meant to her.

Somehow she managed to free him from his shirt, as he managed to free her from her dress, from her bra, from her slip, igniting more of those fires with each touch of his hands, of his lips, of his tongue.

"Evan..." She was incapable of saying more than his name, but knew she had to tell him what he made her feel, how much she wanted him, how she wanted him to need her as much as she needed him. "Evan..."

With trembling fingers she reached for his belt buckle. She felt him go suddenly still above her, waiting. Fumbling only slightly, she opened the belt and released his zipper, reaching to find the warm satin strength of him.

"Oh, Anna," he said on an indrawn breath, and then restraint was gone—his and hers. Their remaining clothes were removed as they both sought to satisfy needs. At last with a smooth, powerful stroke, he joined them.

She looked up at him, his face once again gilded by lamplight and thought she would never see a more beautiful sight. She felt the tremors beginning inside her as he began moving within her and surrendered to the all encompassing cataclysm of Evan Claymore's love, hearing his cry as he, too, surrendered and joined her in a world where everything was beautiful, where anything was possible, where, at last, they were together.

Long minutes later, he rolled to one side, taking her with him, holding her close as their heartbeats and breathing returned to something approaching normal.

He hugged her closer, tightening his arms around her, then drew a deep breath and pulled away so that he could look into her eyes.

"I do love you, Anna," he said with quiet, almost desperate intensity, so at odds with the warm lethargy she had felt until he spoke. "And if you will trust me to treasure you," he continued, "I promise that I will love you forever. Will you trust me, Anna?"

Evan lifted his hand to Anna's face, capturing it and looking deep into her eyes while waiting for her answer. And Anna, who had once abandoned all hope of ever hearing those words, who had grown to love Evan while hiding behind yards of bandages, who even yet was startled when she saw her new face in the mirror, looked deep into Evan's eyes, beyond the surface of this man whom she once thought so confident, into his heart, where she saw the loneliness of his life without her and the truth of his words.

Now she willed him to be able to see into her with all the perception he had shown in the past, because only that way could she convince him of the truth of her feelings. But if he didn't believe her now, she knew that one day he would. She smiled at him, gently, with her eyes, with her lips, and with her heart, hiding her fleeting sadness at not yet having convinced him, promising him a lifetime of all the love she had stored up for years while she waited, just for him.

"Yes," she whispered. "And I will treasure you."

Epilogue

—

Anna lay alone in Jed Claymore's massive oak bed. An errant June breeze ruffled the lace curtains covering the tall windows and danced its way over her satin-and-lace-clad body.

She twisted and shifted, trying to get comfortable, but she knew that was hopeless. No matter what position she took, she'd never rest easy unless Evan was beside her.

The house was quiet. The servants—and there were a few, now, to care full-time for the house and gardens—had long ago left for their homes or retired to their rooms.

Jane wasn't among them. Nor was she anywhere in the house, or Anna would have been tempted to wake her for a quiet talk. But Jane had decided her role would be that of favorite aunt, or maybe surrogate grandmother at some later date. And she'd also decided she really liked managing Anna's shop.

By taking over the routine chores, as well as most of the burden of seeing to customers, Jane had freed Anna to devote time to her clay, and, with increasing frequency, to her sculpture.

She glanced at the table on Evan's side of the bed. She'd thought to surprise him, hours ago, when she had placed the finished sculpture there. The body of it had been finished for months. They had taken the plaster cast to the foundry within weeks of returning from their honeymoon, and she had waited, white-knuckled, to learn if her bracing had held or if the fragile wing had shattered during the pouring process. But only today had she completed and assembled all the other work—the stem, the leaves, the walnut base, and the brass plaque.

Chrysalis, she had called the sculpture in its official title. She rose up in the bed and reached over to touch the polished bronze wing. But in private...

The flare of headlights cut across the night sky outside her windows, and Anna grinned. "It's about time," she said, patting the wing once more and setting the delicate cocoon to swaying gently.

Evan had his tie and his jacket off and his shirt unbuttoned by the time he swept into the bedroom. He was still the sexiest man she had ever seen, but there ended any comparison with the imperious man she had first seen walking in on her while she lay in another kind of bed.

For one thing, he paid attention to her this time. He tossed his tie and jacket onto a chair as he crossed the room, coming directly to her side and dropping down onto the edge of the bed.

"How are—"

He smothered her words in his mouth as he gathered her in his arms. How she loved him when he was masterful, she thought, surrendering to his magic. How she loved him, period. He pulled away from her with a noisy, smacking kiss and lowered his lips to her stomach. "And hello to you, too, little Jed," he said, punctuating the words with a gentle tap of his knuckles to her swollen abdomen.

"Oh, Evan, don't wake him up again," Anna moaned, laughing in spite of the vigorous kick that answered Evan's summons. Little Jed had been conceived in this bed, where Great-great-grandma and Great-great-grandpa had created nine babies. She and Evan had both agreed that nine might be a few too many but that they both had enough love stored up to nourish even a house this size full of little Claymores.

"And you—" He looked at her, smiling, love and wonder and joy of living shining from his eyes. "Don't you ever let me go off and leave you for another overnight trip. I don't care how important the board says it is."

"Yes, sir. But if you would just get busy and bring that board to Fort Smith, you wouldn't have to go away at all."

He slid down in the bed beside her, holding her close. "Soon," he promised. "Tell me you missed me."

"I brought you something," she said instead.

"Tell me you missed me," he growled, placing a possessive hand over her breast. "Then tell me you love me. And then maybe I'll be in the mood to talk about some *thing*."

He was teasing her. She knew he loved every present she gave him, because he knew that each one of them came from her heart.

"I missed you," she said, placing a kiss on his forehead. "I love you. Now look at your nightstand."

Evan raised his head and looked, at first humoring her, then with genuine interest. "You finished it." He eased up from her and walked around the bed, kneeling to touch the base of the sculpture.

She watched him kneeling there, looking at her work with awe, and she thought of the morning she had started that work. She'd gone into her studio to hide herself in creation. She'd hoped she'd find Evan in the wax, but when the butterfly emerged she'd thought she'd been given some metaphor for herself. Evan had thought so, too.

What she hadn't realized, and what he might never realize, was that the metaphor had not been for her.

No, the plaque should read *Evan.* Or maybe *Love.*

"Evan?"

"Mmmm?" he said, turning from the statue, tugging off his already unbuttoned shirt, toeing off his shoes.

"Did you miss me? Do you love me?"

"Always, my love."

She smiled at him provocatively. She was working on her leer, but she wasn't quite sure she'd mastered it. "Well, aren't you going to show me how much?"

He grinned—*his* leer was perfect, as was the rest of him— and slid into the bed, taking her in his arms. "Always, my love."

And he did.

*   *   *   *   *

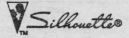

Take 4 bestselling love stories FREE

Plus get a FREE surprise gift!

Special Limited-time Offer

Mail to Silhouette Reader Service™

3010 Walden Avenue
P.O. Box 1867
Buffalo, N.Y. 14269-1867

YES! Please send me 4 free Silhouette Desire® novels and my free surprise gift. Then send me 6 brand-new novels every month, which I will receive months before they appear in bookstores. Bill me at the low price of $2.44 each plus 25¢ delivery and applicable sales tax, if any.* That's the complete price and—compared to the cover prices of $2.99 each—quite a bargain! I understand that accepting the books and gift places me under no obligation ever to buy any books. I can always return a shipment and cancel at any time. Even if I never buy another book from Silhouette, the 4 free books and the surprise gift are mine to keep forever.

225 BPA ANRS

Name	(PLEASE PRINT)	
Address	Apt. No.	
City	State	Zip

This offer is limited to one order per household and not valid to present Silhouette Desire® subscribers. *Terms and prices are subject to change without notice.
Sales tax applicable in N.Y.

UDES-94R

Fifty red-blooded, white-hot, true-blue hunks
from every State in the Union!

Look for MEN MADE IN AMERICA! Written by some of
our most popular authors, these stories feature fifty of the
strongest, sexiest men, each from a different state in the
union!

Two titles available every month at your favorite retail
outlet.

In July, look for:

ROCKY ROAD by Anne Stuart (Maine)
THE LOVE THING by Dixie Browning (Maryland)

In August, look for:

PROS AND CONS by Bethany Campbell (Massachusetts)
TO TAME A WOLF by Anne McAllister (Michigan)

You won't be able to resist MEN MADE IN AMERICA!

SILHOUETTE® Desire®

Big Bad WOLFE

WOLFE WATCHING
by Joan Hohl

Undercover cop Eric Wolfe knew *everything* about divorcée Tina Kranas, from her bra size to her bedtime—without ever having spent the night with her! The lady was a suspect, and Eric had to keep a close eye on her. But since his binoculars were getting all steamed up from watching her, Eric knew it was time to start wooing her....

WOLFE WATCHING, Book 2 of Joan Hohl's devilishly sexy Big Bad Wolfe series, is coming your way in July...only from Silhouette Desire.

IT'S OUR 1000TH SILHOUETTE ROMANCE, AND WE'RE CELEBRATING!

JOIN US FOR A SPECIAL COLLECTION OF LOVE STORIES
BY AUTHORS YOU'VE LOVED FOR YEARS, AND
NEW FAVORITES YOU'VE JUST DISCOVERED.
JOIN THE CELEBRATION...

April
REGAN'S PRIDE by **Diana Palmer**
MARRY ME AGAIN by **Suzanne Carey**

May
THE BEST IS YET TO BE by **Tracy Sinclair**
CAUTION: BABY AHEAD by **Marie Ferrarella**

June
THE BACHELOR PRINCE by **Debbie Macomber**
A ROGUE'S HEART by **Laurie Paige**

July
IMPROMPTU BRIDE by **Annette Broadrick**
THE FORGOTTEN HUSBAND by **Elizabeth August**

SILHOUETTE ROMANCE...VIBRANT, FUN AND EMOTIONALLY
RICH! TAKE ANOTHER LOOK AT US! AND AS PART OF THE
CELEBRATION, READERS CAN RECEIVE A FREE GIFT!

YOU'LL FALL IN LOVE ALL OVER
AGAIN WITH
SILHOUETTE ROMANCE!

CEL1000